RETRIBUTION

James Napier served as an officer in the British Army in the late 1980s and early 1990s, including an operational tour in South Armagh, Northern Ireland. Stints selling caviar in Mayfair, clearing landmines in Afghanistan, gaining an MBA from Edinburgh University, working in the Borders knitwear industry and various start-up companies in London, preceded a move to Norfolk where he has settled with his family and a career in telecoms. He was also educated at Eton and the Royal Military Academy Sandhurst.

Retribution is his first published novel. A second novel, also set in Afghanistan and featuring Piers Walker is nearing completion.

RETRIBUTION

James Napier

RETRIBUTION

Olympia Publishers
London

www.olympiapublishers.com
OLYMPIA PAPERBACK EDITION

Copyright © James Napier 2007

The right of James Napier to be identified as author of
this work has been asserted in accordance with sections 77 and
78 of the Copyright, Designs and Patents Act 1988

All Rights Reserved

No reproduction, copy or transmission of this publication
may be made without written permission.
No paragraph of this publication may be reproduced,
copied or transmitted save with the written permission of the
publisher, or in accordance with the provisions
of the Copyright Act 1956 (as amended).

Any person who does any unauthorized act in relation to
this publication may be liable to criminal
prosecution and civil claims for damage.

A CIP catalogue record for this title is
available from the British Library

ISBN: 978-1-905513-30-7

This is a work of fiction.
Names, characters, places and incidents originate from the
writers imagination. Any resemblance to actual persons, living or
dead, is purely coincidental.

First Published in 2007

**Olympia Publishers
60 Cannon Street
London
EC4N 6NP**

Printed in Great Britain

To my parents

*'There are four good legs to my father's chair,
People and Priests, Land and Crown
I sits on all of them fair and square
And that's the reason it don't break down.'*

Rudyard Kipling

Chapter 1

Autumn 1990 – South Armagh

Lance Corporal Stephen Hill's last sight was of a little owl silhouetted against a blazing autumn dawn. It sat quietly in the top of a long-dead oak tree, watching intently as the twelve heavily laden Guardsmen pushed their way along the overgrown and muddy track. A chorus of chirruping from the wood piped the patrol on its way, steaming in the cool damp. The owl lifted its shoulders, shivered its feathers and leaning slightly forward blinked at the young Lance Corporal.

A smile appeared on Hill's camouflaged face, which was streaked with sweat from the morning's three mile detour to the pick-up-point. The owl was a lovely sight to end the patrol, he thought, and at Bessbrook Mill there'd be a warm room, a bath, a breakfast he hadn't had to cook and a quick call to his girlfriend.

Death may merely be a moment in life, but in that moment Stephen Hill's life was vaporised. The force of the five-hundred-pound home-made explosive bomb of fertiliser compound was directed between his neck and ankles from only four feet away. The massive explosion scythed an arc of destruction through the wood, sending a dozen trees crashing to the ground, their branches stripped off by the blast. The noise carried for twenty miles and the impact for five.

The patrol was flung to the ground; time was reduced to half-speed. Second Lieutenant Piers Walker, barely one year out of Sandhurst, lay on his belly, his forty-five-pound rucksack shoved uncomfortably against his helmet, his face forced into the grime of the footpath. His head rang like a cathedral bell. He raised it with a jerk, and the rucksack subsided down his sweaty back. He pulled his SA-80 rifle towards him and took up the semblance of a fire position with one hand. His left hand reached for the prestel switch of the microphone clipped to the top of his webbing. His voice was clear and unshaken, his heart thudding, fit to explode.

'Hello Zero, this is Yankee Two-Zero-Alpha. Contact now, close to pick-up. A loud explosion. Wait-out.'

'Zero – roger. Out,' came the sanitised reply from HQ back at Bessbrook.

No amount of pyrotechnics in the training camps back in Kent could have prepared him for this. This was real. This was South Armagh – Bandit Country. He was on his own now. The lives of his patrol were in his hands. Piers Walker smiled to himself, as if to bolster his courage.

He leaned back onto his right shoulder and shouted, 'Stay exactly where you are. Look out for enemy movement to your front.' His clipped public school accent was firm. It was what he wanted to hear, and what his men needed to hear. 'Lance Sergeant Rothwell, are you okay?'

'Aye, Sir,' a resolute, slightly exuberant Geordie voice bellowed back.

'Are the men all right?'

Jimmy Rothwell, at twenty-two a Lance Sergeant of two years, and the next in seniority to Piers Walker, was the lead man of the last of three teams of four. Positioned some one hundred and fifty yards from the front of the patrol, Jimmy raised himself to project his voice and called each man's name. One name went unanswered. Piers reached for the microphone again.

*

Martin Finnan had known that the patrol was spending the night on his ground – his collie dogs had told him so. The 'dickers' had followed their every move like a shadow between Newtownhamilton, Belleek and Silverbridge, and had told him to expect them. His dogs had also told him that the patrol had moved off just before dawn.

Roused, he stepped out of bed and put on his long Gaelic Football socks. He stretched his 5'4" stout body, placed both hands on his belly – which amply filled his pink long johns – and gave it a satisfying jiggle. He grinned a yellow gappy-toothed grin at himself in the mirror and stroked his white beard. In the kitchen he made a mug of tea, turned on the radio and looked at the dawn peeping into the darkness. The dogs had stopped barking; the patrol had moved away from his property. He had time. He made some toast. He put on his soiled blue dungarees and wellingtons, grabbed a faded red Massey Ferguson baseball cap and left the house, leaving the kitchen light on.

From the shed he took a sack of sheep nuts, and let his two collies out of their kennel. They crouched beside him, wheeling and turning at his heels. He threw the sack into the open back of his red Toyota pickup truck.

'Get hup!' he said to the dogs, barely opening his mouth.

Dawn was beginning to win its battle from the east and the night was in retreat, leaving a rearguard of dark blue and emerald to fight on. He turned on the engine, lights and the radio and headed north.

Five miles on he stopped. He looked down into a shallow bowl of small fields in which the light had begun to pick out the first stirrings of livestock. He left the engine running and the fan blowing warm air onto his feet. In the glove box he found an outwardly ragged pair of Zeiss binoculars, with bailer twine as a strap. Putting them to his eyes he squinted, adjusting the focus. He moved up through his field – neglecting his ewes – to a thick block of forestry and set his focus. He happened upon a tall, lifeless oak tree, the tallest tree there, and in its top he saw a little owl serenely snoozing.

'Ar, 'tis a wonderful ting, murther nature,' he muttered to himself as he replaced his binoculars and jumped out of the cab.

He was suddenly distracted from his livelihood by the sight of the little owl's flight from its perch, staggering as if drunk, and then dropping like a sycamore pod to the open ground between himself and the wood. Almost at once a pall of grey smoke swallowed up his ancient perch, and the trees around it trembled and fell silently like dominoes.

Then he heard and felt the blast, knocking him off his feet, and sending the dogs spinning and yelping in a wild fury; the sheep splayed motionless on the turf. Slowly he gathered himself up onto his elbows and rubbed his face. He picked up his cap from beside the Toyota and pulled himself up by the gate. His head still shook from the blast. He looked across the bowl to the forest and saw the great cloud of smoke and debris hanging over it like a headstone. All manner of terrified fowl circled around it, like chaff from a bonfire.

He looked for the soldiers on the hillock opposite, one mile away, then to the edge of the wood but he saw no sign of life. He stepped inside the gate and called for his dogs as the first of three helicopters came into view from the east.

*

Piers Walker's multiple climbed aboard the Wessex helicopter. As he got on he glanced across at Jimmy Rothwell, and smiled faintly. Now it was over, exhaustion and shock had begun to overcome the adrenaline. Piers looked out of the open doorway and down. He could see the wood below, smouldering. It was as if its heart had been surgically removed. He shut his eyes. Even squeezing them tight could not expunge what they had seen, what they had touched and what they had smelt. He wiped his hands on his combat trousers, front and back. Peeping he saw still the stain of blood on his hands. The blood of a young man under his command. A dead young man.

Jimmy had taken him to the scene, a conical earthen crater flanked by violently broken tree stumps, like fangs. A thickening layer of milky whiteness was rising from the ground. The wood was still. Twigs snapped underfoot, causing them to pull their rifle stocks more firmly into their shoulders. The wood smelt of freshly turned earth, combined with the rank sweetness of crude homemade explosives. They'd stood silently, awed by the carnage and with eyes darting, picking up every movement of the wood settling back on its wounds. And then they'd seen it; hanging from a stripped branch fifty yards away. A helmet, dangling from its chinstrap.

A mulch of pummelled brains and skull dripped from it. Impulsively Piers had stooped to touch it and recoiled in horror at its warmth. From the pit of his stomach he'd let out a cry of pain.

Now he held his head in hands. It could have been worse. It did not cross his mind that it could have been him. He looked up, and with shame and fear inhabiting the hollow of his soul he glimpsed the ashen, callow faces of his soldiers. Three days before, a group of twelve confident young men had set out on patrol in an area that they had perhaps grown too accustomed to. Now eleven were returning to base; eleven frightened young boys.

*

It took Martin Finnan twenty minutes to get home. He left the dogs in the back of the pickup and went into the kitchen and listened to the radio as he pulled off his boots. His mug of tea was half full but stone cold; he drank it off in one. The elation of the attack was seeping away and for the first time in his solitary life an oft-suppressed doubt was bubbling to the surface, probing his morality: *What was the point in killing some nineteen-year-old who'd simply been sent to obey orders? Wasn't it all just playing at war, simply a relief from the poverty and boredom as he tended his smallholding?*

He remembered the sneer of his cousin, a rich property developer in Dublin: *"Still playing at cowboys and Indians, eh, Mart?"* Martin had never spoken to him again. Anger and hatred welled up as his resolve returned at the memory. No. He'd never abandon his friends, nor the fight against the Brits who'd stolen his ancestors' land and still swaggered around as though he were their servant.

But still he found himself longing more and more for the first whiskey of the evening, and the ebullience he showed to his comrades became more of an act. He braced himself as he picked up the telephone and dialled a number from memory.

'Hello, would tat be Sean?' he said.

'Aye, 'tis that, Mart, you auld tramp you, and what can I be doing for yoursel,' the voice replied.

'Well now, I taught tat youse might be interest'd in a little turf news today. I tink that I've got jus da one winner for you.'

'Aye, well, you'd be wastin' your time terre, Mart. I gave up tat malarkey long, long ago. Goodbye to you.'

Sean Connor put down the receiver and tapped the living room table with his folded Racing Post. A little smile broke across his cadaverous, haunted face, momentarily disguising the two three-inch scars that traced their way from the corner of his left eye across his temple. He pushed his scraggy brown hair up with a soil-ingrained hand, whose fingers were split and coarse through manual labour on the council roads. He sniffed emphatically through his oft broken, hooked nose, looked out of the window at the statue in Crossmaglen Square, and finished his tea swiftly. He stuffed the Racing Post into his donkey jacket, grabbed his car keys from the hall table and left his house by the back door.

MAP OF SOUTH ARMAGH

Chapter 2

Autumn 1993 – South Armagh

It was two o'clock in the morning. The light drizzle was picked out, like a haze, in the sickly-yellow neon lighting of Bessbrook helipad. The young Fusilier sentry kicked lazily at the kerbstone. He was alerted from his sloth by the first of sixteen men, split equally into four groups. Silently they filed past, the sentry staring after them in awe. The size of the men was not noticeably different to his own regiment, though the strong, quiet professionalism and the bulk that they bore were immense by comparison.

A wind of curiosity had preceded the men to the tiny Buzzard Operations Room, where four clean white faces were pressed against the glass. Outside, three men taking a cigarette break watched the procession. An array of weaponry could be discerned: a pair of M19 grenade launchers and two .50 Browning tripods pinning their carriers like yoked oxen, the barrels resting easily on two broad shoulders. Each man cradled his steely grey and careworn G3 rifle in his right arm. Four of the men also carried the standard-issue British Army rifle in their left arms, giving the impression of water diviners. Every second man carried a five-gallon jerrycan of water. Faces were painted black, the eyes alert and focused.

In the distance the distinct *bugh-bugh-bugh* of a Chinook helicopter beat the inky sky, getting louder before suddenly swooping down onto the helipad. The tailgate lowered and a green fluorescent light stick beckoned each chalk forward into its belly. The men slipped their vast carapaces over one shoulder and advanced in order.

Underneath the Chinook the ground staff secured two underslung loads of palleted sandbags.

The tailgate rose, and the Chinook lifted gently, then lunged forward heading eastwards into the dawn. As it gained height the sky glowed, reflecting the distant lights of Newry. How jolly and seductive they looked from above, thought Trooper Barry Ferguson, staring out of the tailgate as the Chinook turned sharply to the south, hugging the border with the Republic.

Ferguson was a solitary countryman at heart, to whom cities had always held a false allure. Too many of his friends had been changed by them – not all for the worse he had to admit – but all had forgotten their roots. His upbringing on his father's sheep farm in the Yorkshire Dales had given him a healthy respect for nature, the land and one's community. He had lived an isolated life by contemporary standards but was by no means dulled towards modern society. The army – which he had joined on leaving school with two A-levels – had shaken off some of this inherent distrust.

Ferguson was the younger of two brothers; the eldest had taken to the land. Though he knew that farming would be his destiny, he first felt the need to explore for himself what his mind had been opened to. The army was an obvious outlet for a physically strong young man, but once within its fold he found that he enjoyed the camaraderie and physical challenges, the responsibility of looking after others. It came as naturally to him as looking after his father's sheep. In his quiet way he had found that he was damned good at it and could forge a career for himself.

He had flown through the ranks of his Guards regiment, had been decorated for bravery in Northern Ireland, and at the age of thirty had succeeded in joining the SAS with whom he was now engaged on this mission in South Armagh. His whole squadron, G-Squadron, was being deployed on what was the largest undercover operation since the Troubles had begun.

Ferguson looked around at the impassive, stoic faces of his colleagues in the ambient light. He smiled to himself as he saw the awed and excitable faces of the two young Fusilier officers who were joining them as liaison officers.

The Chinook headed south-west across the Drumintee bowl and hugged the southern spur of Slieve Gullion, before heading back on itself over the village of Mullaghbane, and then west towards the tinier hamlet of Silverbridge in the very heart of South Armagh. It dropped swiftly, landing in the col of Carrigan's Hill. The tailgate eased down and the sixteen men quickly vacated with all their bulky equipment, fanning out and blown onto their bellies by the downdraft. The underslung loads were disconnected and the Chinook was airborne within a minute.

Three groups of four instantly became two of six, each with a Browning and M19 in the party. The Squadron Commander, Sergeant Major and the two liaison officers were left in the col as the two groups filed off in opposite directions to claim the peaks. The commander looked up as dawn illuminated scudding clouds in an overcast sky.

'It's gonna rain,' he said as he took a map from inside his camouflage smock. He glanced at the two peaks some fifty metres from him and no more than ten metres higher, and then down at the ribbon of streetlights in Silverbridge. 'Better get cracking,' he said to his three colleagues as he replaced his map.

The morning coloured the black canvas that the soldiers had been busying themselves with. The villagers immediately below and to the west stirred. Lights came on in the council houses that flanked the village green. Peat smoke began to drift up from first one, and then every chimney top, as if returning the airy wave of the poncho flapping above them. But the smoke also acted as a marker to those far off that the village had company.

The hill slid steeply and bobbled over craggy outcrops until gently lolling into a lush pasture bounded by drystone walls. Vast dark lollipops of trees stuck out from the ribbon of road that wound its way from north to south and around the hill. The road could not yet be seen in the lightening sky but the leafy deciduous trees guided the troopers' eyes and oriented them to their maps.

It was a dewy morning and the night clung heavily to the whitewashed farm walls directly below the OP, daubing them grey against the cheery yellow windows. Inside, a farmer pulled on his overalls in between swigs of tea. Kennelled dogs began to bark as the front door threw a blob of light into the yard. A man limped across it. He opened the kennel and then swung himself onto an ancient blue tractor, long without its cabin. The tractor shot up smoky mushrooms as it puttered into life and headed west, chased by the dawn and three yapping collie dogs.

Beyond the village the ground extended into a patchwork of small green fields, dotted with pre-fabricated bungalows. The reality was that the area that they looked across was the arena for the most sophisticated of terrorists. The ground rose and dropped: the product of glacial retreat. It was a lattice of minor roads affording the terrorists with many firing points and getaways, and the soldiers with a veritable obstacle course between them. If not every local was a sympathiser to the cause, then most were.

'Youse should see the way those two Ruperts are carrying on down there,' said Trooper Watts as he returned with the last of the sandbags and stamped them into place, whilst Barry Ferguson was making a brew of tea. 'It's as though they're out to impress the in-laws at the first time of meeting 'em.' The six SAS men laughed.

Ferguson smiled as he took a mouthful of hot tea from the black beaker and passed it round. 'Aye, well, they'll not be so chirpy when Paddy starts rainin' lead on 'em.'

'You've bin 'ere before, haven't you, Baz?' said Watts as he took the beaker and cupped it in his hands.

'Aye,' he replied, as he stared through the post box between canopy and sandbags.

'Weren't you caught by a landmine a couple o' years back?'

'Aye – well not exactly meself – but the Boss, young Piers, he was. He was in charge of the multiple that got hit. Me, I was on the hill guarding the HLS. And Jimmy Rothwell, he was with Piers as well.' He kept his watch, not turning to Watts who knew the story full well. But not everyone did, and another, Tom Skilling, a Glaswegian, coaxed him on.

'So what happened?'

'We were on our way home after four days tramping about. We were almost there – I could've sworn I'd heard the choppers coming in for us – when all of a sudden – BOOM!' He paused for effect. 'Corporal Hill bought the whole package. Only found small pieces of him. They'd been clever – damned clever – but then they are, aren't they? We had two months to go after that and were crapping ourselves every time we went out.' His eyes misted over at the thought of that day, still raw and yet so distant now, and with the Gulf War in between.

'How did the Boss take it?'

'Well he's a strong 'un is Piers, and so young at the time – only twenty-one I reckon. Kept his cool. Pulled 'em together and got them back to BBK. It was him and Jimmy that went back to look for Stevie. The boys adored Piers anyhow, but they respected him more from that day onwards. They say it made him – but I say that he is the man he is by any road. But I know it hurt him deep down.'

Silence overcame the group, save for the tap-tap-tapping on the other summit of the last preparations of their two gun pits. Beneath them, crows in the treetops stirred and cawed to each other.

'Did you know who did it?' asked Tom Skilling quietly.

'Aye, we did that, Tom.' He accepted the now tepid beaker as it came round. 'And we made a pact that day that we'd get the bastard.' He swallowed the last of the tea and shook out the dregs.

*

Inside the van, Piers Walker was feeling a little nervous. He remembered reading in *War and Peace* how Nicholai Rostov rode into battle for the first time against the French, telling himself that it was best to feel slightly afraid, so that your nerves were more alert. Now he knew what Tolstoy had meant. The IRA ambush that had killed Stephen Hill had taught him that war offered nothing like the glamour of a uniform or the excitement of the Boy's Own escapades that he'd imagined. Yet the whole experience had drawn him into seeking more action.

He heard three knocks from the driver and gave a single knock in reply. The van was slowing to take the first corner of the sharp S-bend.

Piers Walker slipped his rucksack over his right shoulder, took hold of his G3 rifle, opened the rear doors and jumped out into the night, landing hard on the soft grassy verge. He watched his three companions debouch in the same manner, silhouetted against the van's break lights. He heard the thud of heavily laden men land on turf, and watched the van disappear over the brow of a slight rise as the Fusilier in the back closed the rear doors. All was silent and dark again. Each man climbed over the drystone wall and crouched behind it. So far, so good, thought Piers.

It was as the aerial photograph and as they had rehearsed the drop off. He took out a pencil torch and a map from inside his smock and sheltered the light with his body. He had recognised the S-bend, and seen the rise that the van dropped beneath, and behind him he could see a small clump of scrub trees. It was enough to confirm that they were at the correct drop-off-point.

He raised himself on his right knee and scanned the area with his CWS night sight. There was no one about, of that he felt confident, but it was reassuring to be certain. He picked out a fox across a small cleft in the ground cut by a stream. The fox stood still, sniffing the air from their general direction and then with a startled jump scampered away into a pocket of scrub. Piers finished his reconnaissance and pulled on his rucksack. With his left hand barely extended from his body, he signalled the direction they would take. Jimmy Rothwell answered with an affirmative grin exposing his strong white teeth, and they moved silently forward.

*

    In a secluded farmhouse in the tiny enclave of Kilcurry across the Irish border, Declan Murphy sat at his kitchen table watching the clock above his stove ticking by. He was a big man with neat black hair framing rosy, but slightly puffy cheeks – the first signs of crossing the watershed of his prime. He wore working dungarees, oil stained about the cuffs, elbows and his thighs from wiping his hands. His thick discoloured white socks steamed, leaving a damp impression on the orange linoleum floor as he shifted his position impatiently.

    Pat McCroy leant against the sink and stared out of the window towards the Daaikilmore Hill across the border. His thoughts took him beyond the physical boundary to his mother in Cullyhana preparing his tea and wondering when he would be home; to his father serving a life sentence for the murder of an RUC constable in Crossmaglen, and to the newly settled grave of his baby brother Joe, killed by the British two years ago. Pat McCroy was twenty-two, with so much personal history, experience and hatred of the British that he was old before his time. The temporal meant little to him – the struggle everything – and from which he could see only one outcome. He sensed that Declan was getting tense. He turned his head, saw that he was right and returning to his musings he smiled: Everyone has their own time, he thought.

    A short, weasel-faced man with a pointy nose, and a boss eye to complete the picture of cherubic beauty, paced nervously up and down the kitchen. After every second patrol he would sit down at the table and sip his tea. Then, after rubbing his sweating palms on the navy blue Guernsey jumper that his mother had knitted him when he was a boy, he'd jump up again and begin his cat-like prowl.

'Damn you, Weasel; will ya not stop your pacing. You're beginning to stiff me. And *damn* Sean Connor, the bastard will be late even for his own funeral.' Declan Murphy's face hardened as the Weasel meekly resumed his seat.

Five minutes passed in brittle silence, the Weasel staring at his empty teacup, Murphy at the clock and McCroy at the hills. The kitchen door opened and in marched Sean Connor, his black donkey jacket flapping, and the Racing Post protruding grubbily from its inside pocket.

'Had a little business to be takin' care o', Declan; I'm sorry to be holding ya up.' He helped himself to a mug of tea from the pot warming on the stove, and then pulled up a chair at the table. 'Well den now what's de crack, boys?'

McCroy looked at Sean. He admired the brazenness of the man in holding up the head of the South Armagh Brigade in his own home without a perceptible care in the world. McCroy knew that the two men went back a long way together, and had played no mean part in establishing the fearsome reputation of the Brigade since the troubles began. Whilst Murphy had grown in stature within the IRA due to professionalism, dependability and a measure of ambition, Sean had always been content to play the foot soldier, though he took advantage of the patronage of those who had risen above him along the way.

'Damn your little business, Sean. If you spent half as much time on dis job rather dan studying de form of dose imperialist's horses de war would long since 'a been won – an' maybe you'd be owning dem horses rather than keeping the bookies in business. Now gentlemen, dat I have everyone's full attention let's get down to de matter in hand shall we.

'You'll not be short of noticing dat we've some unwanted company about Silverbridge. Now de man wants rid o' dem. He wants rid of dem 'cause der der, and 'cause the boys in the smoke tink that we're going soft on 'em down 'ere. Now we know dat a Chinook landed der dis mornin', and we know dat it was carrying a good deal of sand 'ith it, which you don't do if you're planning a fleeting stopover. We know dat dey've a position up on de hill, and we know what dey can see fra der. So I sent Seamus and Colin to have a wee look for us, an' some of de boys'll take a wee look in the hedgerows a'ter dat.' He paused, frowning at Connor. 'An' now we're all here, all we have to do is wait.'

McCroy turned to Connor and grinned before remarking, 'You'll be remembering Carrigan's Hill den will you, Sean?'

'Oh, you're a hoot a minute you are, boy, I'll tell ya ya no'd be laughing if 'twere you ya little bastard.' As he retorted he rubbed the scar tissue on his left temple. Three years previously the Royal Marines had set up an OP on Carrigan's Hill only for it to be attacked within a week, forcing its withdrawal. In the gunfight, Sean Connor had the narrowest of escapes when a bullet smashed the stock of his AK47 and the splinters gauged the skin around his left temple, leaving him permanently scarred.

Unwilling to open a mouth filled with rotten gappy teeth, the Weasel spoke with a nasal drawl: ''Twas through Silverbridge mysel dis morn, and saw de boys on de hill up der. It seemed to me to be a mighty obvious ting to be doing, ya know. You could see de OP for afar off. It don't seem right to me – a bit fishy if you ask me.'

'Well let's jus wait 'n see what de boys come back wit, shall we. Now, Sean, be a good lad an' stick de kettle back on to boil now will ya.'

Chapter 3

Thin wisps of smoke drifted eastwards from the twin peaks of Carrigan's Hill before disappearing like the lingering vapour from a sunken steamship's funnels. Piers Walker rested his binoculars and chuckled enviously to himself. What he wouldn't give for a hot brew and to stretch his legs. For nearly two days his team of four had barely moved from their lying-up position; not a word had been spoken between them in this time, and they had relied upon cold rations for sustenance, and plastic bags and bottles for constitutional needs.

Piers glanced over to his right and watched the sun begin to drop swiftly from the day, giving way to a vast orange inferno. He remembered his English teacher at school remarking upon a similar sunset seen through his study window, quoting from the Rubaiyat of Omar Khayyam:

> *For in and out, above, about, below,*
> *'Tis nothing but a magic Shadow-show*
> *Play'd in a Box whose Candle is the Sun,*
> *Round which we Phantom Figures come and go.*

His reflections lingered on his school days, where he, at the innocent age of eight, had been subjected to the bullying taunts and beatings of the larger boys. Through his snivelling tears he had vowed that he would command the same awe and respect when he filled out. When the time came all he saw was fear and resentment in the squits that he had set upon, and through that the futility of being a bully. As a school prefect he had exacted a cathartic revenge on those whom he knew to be bullies. He felt a symmetry of intent in the specific operation he was now engaged in.

At the base of the slope the mist was fast and thickly gathering, filling the hollows. From within its confines he heard the shouts of a man calling his dogs. Nothing unusual in that, this after all is farming country. Then he heard the tap-tap-tapping of a walking stick against a wire-fence, stonework and hedgerow, and descried through the fog the dogs' owner urging them to search out the ditch as if trying to put up a pheasant. Piers firmly knocked Jimmy Rothwell's right foot with his left. The signal went round the team and came back to his right foot. The G3s were pulled tightly, expectantly, into shoulders.

From out of the mist and heading along the road parallel to their position, a tall, ginger bearded man emerged wearing a black trench coat flapping open with his exertions, to reveal a grey sweatshirt, working blue denim jeans and black wellington boots. With his right hand he vigorously beat at the hedgerows with an ash-pole, and on his head, pushed back, he wore a navy blue woollen bobble hat. Two black and white spaniels rambled loyally ahead of him, pausing every now and then to sniff the fast dewing ground. In the corner of the field the dogs wheeled round, awaiting instructions. Piers saw the man flick his stick and then heard him prompt his dogs to continue to search: 'Heed on!'

One dog leapt onto the stone wall and like a trapeze artist, began to make his way up the hill, teetering and then eventually throwing himself to the ground as though he meant to do so. The other dog stayed on the same side of the wall and sprinted off in the direction of Piers' team.

Piers and Jimmy looked on – every sense taut as the dog moved closer to them. They had not been down to the road, or approached their hideout from it, and what little wind there was came from the south-east towards them. Each reasoned therefore, that the dogs could not be following their scent. Their position was not an obvious one, being too far from the road for a conventional roadblock. However, for the element of counter-surprise and the firepower that they had, the position was perfect. The beater must realise this if he were doing his job correctly.

Piers watched the onward progress of the dogs, now only one hundred yards away and sure to compromise them. They had no option but to sit tight. To intercept the dogs or to attempt to draw them off could not but alert the beater. Instinctively Piers lowered his blackened face, his head covered with a green woollen cap-comforter, and narrowed his eyes, never straying from the panorama below him. The dogs were fifty yards away, now on either side of the wall. He felt moral support in the two ankles that entwined his but inside his heart quickened.

He heard a car in the mist behind the beater, heading in the same direction. He saw a pair of lights penetrate the whiteness, and then a beige Cortina drew level with the man in the trench coat. The car stopped. The driver leant over to the passenger's side and opened the door. The two men exchanged words. Still the dogs advanced. A booming Irish voice burst through the intense vigil like the first volley from a firing squad.

''Ome way, boys!' cried the beater as he stood facing directly up the hill. It was as though he was staring right into Piers' eyes. The dogs stopped their snuffling advance and turned to their master. ''Ome way, boys!' he called again, this time with a friendlier inflection, and beckoned them with his free hand. The dogs, hunched and frozen, jumped forward and bounded down the hill. The beater vaulted the barbed wire fence and opened the passenger side rear door for his dogs, which charged into the vehicle and settled in the foot-wells, panting furiously with steam emanating from their sodden coats and dripping jowls. The car moved off.

'Did ya see anyting dere, Roy?' said the driver as he reached across to pick up a packet of cigarettes from the open glove compartment and offer his passenger one in passing.

'Na. Nat a ting, Kenny. We worked up de side o' de road from de Silver Bridge until ya saw tus jus now. Me lads picked up no kinda scent at all, an' I saw notin' mesel. How's about yoursel?'

Kenny bent over the wheel with a cigarette in his mouth, his neck extended towards the car's cigarette lighter, held between finger and thumb whilst his other digits clung to the wheel. It was an awkward position but one well practised. He puffed out great clouds with satisfaction and replaced the lighter. He shook his head.

'Likewise, noting doing at all. I driven right around de hill an seen no sign of life. But da man wants us ta drive thru de hill now, an I taught dat you'd do wi' a lift.' He smiled at Roy as he turned the car to the right and then immediately right again, leaving the single tarmac road for a rising dirt track, its cam bearded with brown sedge.

He turned off his lights and drove at five miles per hour through the pass. The peaks on either side were some one hundred to two hundred yards off but only twenty metres higher than the track. Roy craned his neck out of the window for a better view in the fast fading light. Of the peaks he could make no more out than had Seamus or Colin before him, but in the col he could see four men at least, in a rear position huddled round a blue flame from which a white steam was pouring.

*

From beneath his cam-net Barry Ferguson watched the slow progress of Kenny's Cortina as it jolted along the scarred track, brushing the sedge forward like a row of dominoes. He had watched the beater and his dogs tapping out the hedgerows, and seen them being picked up by the Cortina. He could sense the nearness of an attack, the pattern of reconnaissance being typical of the Provisional IRA.

No word had come from the five cut-off groups positioned around the hill of having been compromised, but then you don't always know that you have been until the attack comes. He watched the car turn to the right then down the hill to join the tarmac road before it switched its lights on.

Ferguson cupped his hands around the steaming black mug of oxtail soup. 'That's the last we'll see o' those boys till mornin' I reckon.' He took a swig.

The rain fell lightly on the cam-net as the light turned from grey into a burnt orange, fired from the neon streetlights of the enclave of Silverbridge below. One of the troopers rubbed an oily rag over the Browning machine gun and checked one last time that the gun was locked onto its Final Protective Fire setting, and that the left and right night pegs were visible. Two troopers deployed Claymore mines around the position, whilst the other two, awakened by the Cortina, prepared a hot meal. The rain fell harder, beating a tattoo on the taut poncho above them as the night set in.

In the dark, the ground below became a smooth bowl of black punctured with the glow of fixed lights in farm dwellings, and small hamlets such as Dorsy to the north and Creggan Duff to the south. Vehicle headlights appeared and then disappeared for no apparent reason, only to re-appear some way on, like a moving game of join the dots to map the roads and pull up the contours. The wind forced the rain harder, and obliquely at the hill in waves like a rip tide, before penitently easing off.

The sodden ground seemed to spit back at the rain, at the same time shuddering intolerably in retreat, absorbing the blow. Above the sounds of nature came the unmistakable thud-thud-thudding of a DSHKA trying to strike its mark. The violence was conjoined with the ferocious beam of a spotlight, picking out the OP in the col, its poncho shining with wetness and flapping furiously, as if suppliantly in the wind.

Ferguson's eye was drawn along the beam to its target, beneath which the ground was being ejaculated like a volcanic eruption. Phosphorescent tracer rounds fizzed in the cloying turf, filling the beam with the steam of fire. He could see the rounds beginning to find their mark; he heard the tortured cry of a wounded liaison officer, his arm hanging from its socket by a single ligament.

The trooper on his gun was already engaging with the enemy, issuing controlled bursts along the line of tracer. Though tracer only burns after a few hundred metres, he'd spotted the muzzle flashes of the DSHKA at the end of the line. Ferguson held out the belt of Browning ammunition, feeding it effortlessly into the tray; he could see the tracer rounds deflecting wildly as they struck the tarmac road and the metal firing point, which sparked magnificently.

Two of the troopers set their G3 sights to four hundred metres and fired two magazines of tracer in rapid bursts of two to three rounds into the spotlight, adjusting their aim for the downward trajectory and the fierce westerly wind. The light was extinguished.

But the tracer attracted its own though inaccurate retort as the DSHKA swung its venomous fire onto their peak, rounds striking and shattering the craggy outcrops immediately below. The top of the cone of fire whizzed and pinged overhead.

The M19's *pop-pop-pop* of sustained bursts added to the crescendo of noise and smoking energy that engulfed every fibre of the unit and every inch within the canopy.

Then it was over; a pulse of the rainstorm. The night was filled with the ringing of deadened eardrums, pierced by the nearness of the excruciating cries of a wounded man. In his earpiece Ferguson could hear a controlled English voice giving clarity to the confusion and the chase below. Like a blind man, his eyes were drawn sightlessly to the sounds of the quarry being hunted down. Ferguson smiled.

*

Two silver Mazda hatchbacks blocked the road to the north at the Cortreasla Bridge, which was in the dead ground before Carrigan's Hill. The Cortina peeled off at the right hand fork, its brake lights bursting through the quickening rain onto the misting windscreen of the dumper truck, whose headlights picked out four men, two behind the wheels of their cars and two others in hooded Barbour jackets, hands deep in pockets, stamping the cold from their feet. The two men moved towards the cab of the truck, the lead man rapping on the driver's window.

''Tis as clean as a whistle, Weasel,' he shouted up above the sound of the engine and the rain. The Weasel raised his head and stroked his beard thoughtfully, pinching a grin. Did his father have such a sickening feeling in the pit of his stomach the night he was killed, he wondered? Every day since that night one of the bigwigs from the city had called to break the news to his mother, he had wondered what it had been like: how he'd died, how he'd felt, and even whether in his dying breath he had felt that it was worth it?

He was proud of his father and proud that people looked upon him as a hero. He himself was no hero, he knew that deep down. He was scared – scared of dying, scared of realising the futility of it all. He owed it to his father and to his mother who was destroyed with hatred for the British. He owed it to the IRA who subsidised their livelihood. And he owed it to himself – the Weasel, a figure to be mocked ever since he was a boy with his nasal speech and crooked face. Not tonight – he would not be mocked tonight.

He watched in his side mirror as the man moved to the rear and entered into a discussion with Murphy. Both men checked their watches in the headlights of the rear vehicle, the breath of each silhouetted like cigarette smoke. The foot-soldiers turned on their heels and trotted back to their roadblock, thumping the driver's door as they went, like an encouraging pat on a racehorse in the owners' enclosure before the off.

Each man's eyes slowly became accustomed to the night as the convoy moved off with lights turned off. Murphy pulled down his balaclava, threw off the tarpaulin, and gripped the DSHKA firmly by both pistol grips, swinging and raising the barrel over the bucket's rim. He steadied his body weight, leaning back into the hay, bracing himself between the weapon and the sides. Connor, his balaclava still worn as a hat, busied himself with the ammunition boxes, raising the lids off each, exposing the first few rounds of the top belt over the edge of each box, and positioning them for a swift connection. He clipped a belt of fifty rounds to the belt hanging from the weapon, and moved the two AK47s to lean against the hay behind and beside each of them. The rain increased as the convoy moved slowly on.

The Weasel picked out the landmarks; a large wet grey rock in the blackness on the left hand verge; the end of a farmer's stone wall on the right, six feet from the road. The Cortina quickened and disappeared.

All this Murphy saw too. It was just as he had planned and rehearsed many times. The truck pulled up opposite a chestnut sapling, the lip of the bucket level with a stone wall on the raised right bank. Murphy set the DSHKA along the line of the top of the sapling and a proud fence post on the inside of the wall and locked the weapon. Crouching at his feet, Connor checked his digital watch, pulled his balaclava down and shifted his feet to ease the blood flow. He depressed the light switch on his watch again.

'Ten seconds,' he muttered, 'Five... Four... Three... Two... One...'

The bucket resounded to the splitting cracks of the DSHKA's fire; empty cases bounced off the dampened hay walls and clinked merrily on the tin floor in peels of three to five, then a pause, followed by another burst of noise and energy. The barrel steamed as waves of raindrops expired sibilantly on the hot black metal. Flashes of fire extruded from the muzzle, reflecting back from the stone wall and illuminating the ecstatic eyes and mouth of Murphy as he coaxed his weapon to extirpate the OP. Connor clipped on yet another belt.

Almost at once the DSHKA was being answered by an annihilating cone of fire from the two hillocks, smashing through the stone wall and striking the reinforced bucket. Browning rounds sparked, span and fizzed off, deflecting into the night.

The Weasel had been enjoying the show; it had been like watching the Hogmanay fireworks up on Edinburgh Castle from Princes' Street. Everything had worked to precision: the positioning of the vehicle; the timing of Murphy's engagement and his apparent accuracy; the junction a split second later with the searchlight pinning the OP. Man it was beautiful, he thought; even the rain seemed heaven sent.

The first rounds of the Brownings found the cab, taking the Weasel's head clean off, like the top of a soft boiled egg, covering McCroy with detritus of the consistency of warm pea soup. He ripped off his balaclava, screaming wildly and gasping for air. The Weasel slumped across him oozing sickly, sweet-smelling, coagulating blood into a fast filling pool on his lap. Rounds sparked off the tarmac in front of him, also striking the metal exterior of the cab. He tugged the limp corpse across him and climbed into the driver's seat. The engine had ceased to tick over. Again and again he frantically turned the ignition key, thumping the steering wheel in desperation and blubbing hysterically. He pulled the Weasel back across as he wormed his way into the passenger's seat, retrieved his AK47 from the foot-well, and slipped out into the night teeming with fire and rain.

As the Brownings broke through the wall, striking the bucket, the air was filled with a competing, impending sound of death. High explosive M19 grenades peppered the vehicle fore, aft and either side. Abruptly the searchlight was put out, but only after Murphy had followed the line of tracer fire from the hilltop position. Smoothly, and in spite of material distractions, Murphy had unlocked the DSHKA and swung freely up along the line of the tracer and then through it, like a clay pigeon shoot, firing as he did so in a continuous burst. Connor kept feeding the insatiable DSHKA belt flapping at Murphy's side. In between he beat as forcibly as he could on the cab roof, urging the Weasel to get going.

From behind the bucket came the anguished cry of McCroy, 'It's de Weasel... 'E's dun fur... De engin's knackerred. I sugges you's get de furc oota der. Tis no use... we've bin snared gooth an' propa.'

'D'ya hear dat, Murph?' yelled Connor.

'Aye,' was the impassive retort as he fired off his final rounds. 'I'll cover you, an' see youse bot at Malloy's later on.' Connor belied his age and physique, easily vaulting over the side of the bucket and landing next to the gibbering McCroy.

'No' we're gonna split up. Ya know where y're goin.' He put a consoling hand on McCroy's slimy shoulder. 'Keep to de bank an' ya'll be doin' fine.' With that he gave him a shove. As McCroy crouched up, ready to make a run for it, a grenade landed ten feet away. It knocked him down like a ninepin. Knocked dead it seemed to Connor.

'Murph! Murph! Will ya come away.' A heavy thump to his rear told Connor that he had decided that there was nothing for it but to run. Murphy slapped him on the shoulder and shouted, 'I'll see youse later,' and he was off like a fox escaping a chicken coop.

*

Walker had missed the Cortina driving slowly north along the B30, its headlights turned off and engine muffled by the wind and rain. That there had been no cars on the road since the light had begun to fade nearly an hour ago was not particularly unusual, but the inertia had begun to make him feel uneasy. Had the dicker spotted them after all, or another OP been compromised? Or indeed, was an attack on the hill position imminent?

Out of the corner of his eye, to the left, he saw the Cortina's brake lights some three hundred yards away. Awkwardly he swung his torso round, and pulling off the cover of his night-sight he followed the line of the road until he came upon the stationary vehicle still belching exhaust fumes. He could see two men sitting in the front of the saloon car, and something obviously warm in the back that he could not make out. The driver turned the engine off and lit a cigarette in cupped hands, its lighted tip burning brightly in the green of his night sight.

Before he had time to make a decision, it was made for him. To his front the hilltop OP was picked out by a powerful spotlight like a rabbit caught in a lamper's beam. Tracer rounds pulsed along a determined upward line, deflecting and sparking wildly and obliquely. Then he heard the thud-thud-thudding of a DSHKA, appeased by the rain, but unmistakable and as invigorating as the starter's pistol in the one-hundred yard dash. The hillocks either side of the OP came to life at once, returning venomous phosphorescent beads of fire.

Jimmy Rothwell and Trooper Dailly stealthily left their position in a well-rehearsed drill, running, crouching all the while, just beneath the stone wall, watched by Walker and Trooper Smith. Rothwell stretched steel calthrops across the road and radioed back to Walker to join him as he and Dailly took up fire positions facing north and south along the road. Walker and Smith followed their route. Above their heavy breathing and the radio talk that resulted from the battle, the noise of the DSHKA and the Brownings was being subsumed by the thunderous explosions of high explosive M19 grenades.

'The lead vehicle of the convoy's only three hundred yards up ahead,' panted Walker as he lay down beside Rothwell. 'They may come back to help. They may be part of the getaway plan now that the op's gone belly-up for them.' He wiped the warm sweat from his face. 'If they don't, then so be it. Our task is to hold the road around the firing point.'

The firefight was easing off; the hay in the back of the truck was now alight, illuminating a fierce, jagged plume of smoke being carried away by the wind. The DSHKA was silent.

'One-Zero-Alpha, this is Zero-Alpha. The truck appears to be immobilised. Move your team in to secure it.'

'Zero-Alpha, this is One-Zero-Alpha. Will do. Moving now, leaving calthrops in place. Out.' Walker raised himself from his prone position and shouted across to his team, 'We're to move in now. Rothwell and Dailly, you lead, and we'll cover you. We'll pepperpot into the firing point. Right – Go! Go!' he screamed, his voice filling with intensity.

The Cortina's reverse lights were a surprising intrusion both to the night's illuminations and to Walker's plan. Swerving wildly on the greasy surface the Cortina picked up velocity as it blindly covered the distance.

'Rothwell! Dailly! Go firm! Go firm!' yelled Walker as loudly as he could muster. 'Zero-Alpha, this is One-Zero-Alpha, we've got company. Looks like the lead vehicle of their convoy. Wait out.' The Cortina slued across the calthrops, puncturing all four tyres as it did so and collided, passenger's side on, into the stone wall.

The four SAS men sprang up and covered the Cortina from four sides, the torchlight from their G3s hitting the two men full in the face. Having hit the steering wheel, the driver was bleeding from above the left eye. The passenger sat in apparent stunned apathy, pinned against the wall; two spaniels in the back barked madly in a high pitch, pawing at the unopened windows. Steam sizzled from the hot engine exposed to the elements by the ruptured bonnet.

'Stay exactly where you are,' shouted Walker. 'Put your hands on your heads.'

Numbed, the two men obliged him. 'Zero-Alpha, this is One-Zero-Alpha. We have two men in a beige Cortina at our VCP. Over.'

'Zero-Alpha – keep 'em there. The QRF are en route and will relieve you. Out to you. Hello Two-Zero-Alpha. Over.'

'Send. Over.'

'Move in to secure the firing point. Over.'

'Roger. Out.'

A beam of light from the first Lynx helicopter enveloped the scene around the Cortina, Kenny and Roy now spread-eagled on the shiny wet tarmac covered by the four SAS men. A second Lynx landed on the road a hundred yards to the north, from which six SAS men disembarked, running towards the Cortina, an RUC constable lagging some paces behind clutching his forage cap.

'Zero-Alpha, this is Two-Zero-Alpha. We've got the big man. He was armed but has given himself up. One dead in the cab, and one mortally wounded beside it. Over.'

'Roger. Out.'

A Gazelle helicopter hovered high above, its Army Air Corps pilot studying the ground through powerful night vision goggles. 'Hello Foxtrot Zero-Alpha, this is Victor One-One-Bravo. We've got a runner. Over.'

'Foxtrot-Zero-Alpha – send grid and direction of travel. Over.'

'Roger. Wait – out.'

'Hello One-Zero-Alpha, this is Zero-Alpha – have the QRF taken over yet? Over.'

'One-Zero-Alpha: yes. Over.'

'Roger – out to you. Victor-One-One-Bravo send sitrep. Over.'

'Victor-One-One-Bravo – you've got one man moving on foot west towards grid 962 184, a derelict building off a farm track. Appears to be armed, and is moving gingerly. Over.'

'Foxtrot-Zero-Alpha – roger. Out to you. Foxtrot-One-Zero-Alpha this is Zero-Alpha: bring him in. Over.'

'Roger. Out.' Walker physically gathered his team on the side of the road. 'The runner's making for Cameron's derelict barn. We'll head back up to our OP and see if we can't pick him up from there. Any questions?' There were none, and without pause Walker led his team back up the hill, covering the two hundred yards like a sprinter on a level running track. From this vantage point they could clearly see the ground that the runner was covering. A Lynx had joined the hunt, its spotlight darting across patches of green and wet grey crag, but always failing to hold the man in its beam.

'Rothwell. Dailly. You two make for the scrub in front of the derelict and Smith 'n I'll chase him into you.' The distance to cover was only three hundred yards but interwoven by one blackthorn hedge, at least two stone walls, and a distended rivulet. Like lurchers, the SAS pairs arced left and right, ensnaring the frightened man in a pincer. Their quarry knew the ground, evading Walker and Smith, going as hard as he might, wading in the rivulet, keeping as low in the water as possible to avoid the Lynx's spotlight.

'Army! Stop or I'll shoot you!' screamed Jimmy Rothwell, holding the runner in his torch beam. Exhausted, the fugitive raised sopping, leaden arms, still clasping his AK47 in his right hand. 'Drop the weapon,' enunciated Rothwell deliberately and loudly. The terrorist did as he was told.

Rothwell advanced towards the man, covering him all the while with his G3, his beam interlocked with that of Dailly's. He discerned real fear in the eyes of the terrorist beneath the balaclava, his lips blue from cold and shock. 'On your knees, man!' He sank into the stream. Rothwell forcefully peeled off the balaclava, and recognising his man exclaimed, 'Oh! Sean Connor, ya beauty! It doesn't get any better than this.' He swung the butt of his G3 violently across the right side of the stunned terrorist's face, cracking the cheekbone and felling him with that single blow. Connor slumped on the stream's bank, meekly receiving the kicked blows of three years of pent up anger and emotion.

'What the bloody hell do you think you're doing?' screamed Walker as he ran to break up this one-sided fight. 'What the blazes has got into you, man?'

Rothwell stepped back. He pulled his G3 meaningfully into his shoulder, aiming the weapon at the scarred temple of Connor who was simpering in a sodden heap. 'It's Connor, Boss. Sean Connor.'

Chapter 4

Autumn 2000 – Hawick, Scotland

Piers Walker looked down at the weir from his office window. The first spate waters of the Teviot tumbled and gushed over the gentle slope, creating a muddy froth in the backwash. It would only be a matter of days now before the first run of salmon charged intently upstream to leap over this minor obstacle. He subconsciously raised his right arm in a mock cast, smiling inwardly. Beyond the rooftops of Hawick the green hills were dotted white with sheep cropping the pasture freshened by the late autumn rain. The drooping leaves of horse chestnut trees lining the riverbank glistened in the morning sunshine. Above them, half-heartedly, an opaque rainbow framed his idyllic picture.

Walker's formative years had been spent in the Borders. The sheep, the hills, the river, the people and the industry were in his blood. Like the salmon that returned to the river from whence they came to spawn and to die so he had been drawn back to his homeland.

For the two years since returning he had worked his way round the various departments of his family's knitting firm: from shift work on the factory floor to the design team's studio. He may be the boss's son but he had served an honest apprenticeship and in so doing earned the respect of the workforce, many of whom knew him already by his exploits for the Hawick Young Man's Rugby Club. His father was grooming him to succeed him in three years time, and to become the fifth Walker to run the business since 1815.

It made him proud to take on the mantle of responsibility upon which no small percentage of the community depended. But the winds of change were gathering pace. The industry had to adapt to new techniques and to focus on its core aptitudes if it were to succeed in an increasingly competitive and global market. The baton to be passed to him may in fact be the shitty stick of timely misfortune. He could see it coming but the folk of Hawick remained blind to it, reciting the mantra that *'its aye bin'* therefore it always will be. But it wouldn't.

He turned back to his desk and picked up his notes on the samples presently being knitted. Dark and earnest looking forebears from a Victorian age peered down at him. Heavy gilt frames added to the weight of expectation frowning upon his desk. Opposing them, Walker had neatly lined up platoons, troops, companies and squadrons of photographs of his own achievements. Even now that he had set his mind and ambition to his task, he sometimes felt pulled between them, like some pained Red Indian performing a test of virility. There was a knock at the door.

'Come in, Jock,' he said, shuffling his papers.

'Mornin' squire,' said the grey-bearded knitting manager, his keen hazel eyes engaging Walker's directly, and an affectionate smile parting well groomed bristles as he spoke. Jock Hunter had been Piers' shift manager for the four months he had spent in the factory, and had also coached him to become a tidy scrum half in the Young Man's Club. He had a square, lined forehead and receding, prematurely grey hair for his forty-seven years and high cheekbones. Some said that he had grown his beard to hide his elfish face, but if so the effect had been accentuated.

'Right then, Jock, shall we see what your boys are doing to the spring sample run?' He grinned and ushered Jock out of the office.

Pushing open the heavy double swing-doors to the factory released a cacophony of rhythmic industry. A hundred knitting frames sluished left and right, right and left. Each manoeuvre leaving another line on the many-coloured knitted panels growing discernibly beneath the watchful eyes of the machine operators.

As Walker moved along the aisle between the frames, so the men themselves visibly grew. From the young man in a Rangers top fresh from his apprenticeship, to the middle aged man with a beer gut hanging over the edge of his trouser waistband, itself joining the cascade, and finally the stooping aspect and pinched cheeks of the old man nearing retirement. All wore intent expressions, oblivious to the world beyond the unsynchronised noise of their machines. Most had sallow complexions from the gloomy surroundings of the factory.

The natural light was obstructed from filling the cavernous area by the lanolin-greasy fluff and dust caking the windows. By way of a substitute, long low strip-lights hung from the ceiling above each frame, the shields dripping with intricate webs of detritus. Occasionally men would break their vigil to mend a broken strand of yarn or replace a cone on top of the frame. At the end of a set of twelve panels they would move along the length of their frame, dextrously pulling off their produce like a gardener tending his vegetable patch. It had always amazed Walker how such an archaic, dingy set up could produce the finest knitwear in Scotland.

As they walked on, some of the men smiled and raised their hands in salute. He stopped to tease Stan Moffat, the ever-youthful shop steward, about his team's weekend drubbing at the hands of Rangers. There was a genuine affection between the men and Walker.

The jerry-built office, centrally sited, threw out an inviting blob of yellow light onto the factory floor and promised respite from the noise. Pale green walls were covered with tattered copies of machinery plans and reams of knitting programmes. Two old school desks faced outwards from the far corners, littered with piles of paper overflowing from in-trays. One long workbench took up the left-hand wall with three empty stools beneath it, while an ancient Sanyo radio perched at one end competed to be heard above the noise.

Davie Stott sat behind one of the desks studying the form guide in the Daily Mirror. Robot-like he lifted a fast eroding cheese sandwich to his mouth, the living contours of his three chins moving in parallel as he chewed. At his elbow was a stained mug of coffee, a crinkly skin settled on its top. Aware of Jock's presence, he swung back on his chair, turned the radio down and stuffed the remainder of his elevenses into his mouth.

'Ulloo, boss,' he mumbled through the dough.

'Watch those fingers of yours,' said Jock, as Davie wiped his mouth with the back of his hand. 'Sorry to disturb your break, but I wanted to show the young squire here the programme.'

'Lead on, MacDuff, lead on; don't mind me,' said Davie in his deep Border's accent. 'Ar woz jus finish' off afore takin a wander aboot the flat mesel.' As Jock's shift leader he had worked his way up into this comfortable sinecure that rarely troubled his leadership skills. He tucked the Mirror under one arm, polished off his coffee in one gulp, made his excuses and squeezed himself out of the room.

'He's an old rascal, eh Jock,' said Walker good-humouredly. It wasn't yet his position to restructure the knitting practices. It was a task that he did not relish, though one that must be grappled with if the greater number were to survive. Sometimes he longed for the simplicity of his previous life. It was odd, he had previously reflected how much easier it had been for him to be an arbiter of life or death, as opposed to someone's livelihood. It was as though the material and the temporal had a greater import to others than life itself, and he dare not dispel that illusion.

Jock led him to the knitting programme and explained the position. The plan was on schedule and the quality to the mark. Walker studied it carefully. Across the tannoy system Radio Borders was interrupted by the seductively soothing tones of Molly, the firm's receptionist,

'Would Mr Piers Walker please come to the phone, there's an outside call for him. Mr Piers Walker.'

Walker made his excuses and dialled reception:

'Hello Molly, it's Piers.'

'Gentleman on the phone for you, Piers. Wouldn't give his name.'

'Thanks Molly, put him through please.' There was a pause whilst Molly made the transfer. 'Hello, Piers Walker speaking.'

'Alright Piers? It's Barry here. Listen mate, I can't talk now but watch the six o'clock news tonight. I'll be in touch soon yeah.'

'But Barry, er, what…' But he had gone. Strange, thought Walker, Barry Ferguson had not called him at work before and indeed he had been out of touch for the last six months or so. The last he had heard there was talk of him leaving the army, but to do what he hadn't gathered. He raised his eyebrows, tucked his lips in on themselves in a cogitative manner, and shook his head slightly.

'You alright, squire?' said Jock, drawing him back to the programme.

'Yeah, yeah… fine. Just an old mate.' And with that Jock had his full attention.

*

Situated at the end of a quarter-mile drive, behind a mature belt of pine trees and on a forward slope facing north, Walker had converted one of his father's cattle byres into a cottage where he lived on his own. He liked his own company and kept himself amused in his own fashion. Occasionally his girlfriend Jenny – the French teacher in the secondary school – would stay over; in the winter months he would train with the rugby club or chase elusive sea trout into the night, and in the summer he and Jenny would often camp in the Cheviot Hills.

He pulled up outside and checked his post stuffed into a loose piece of drainpipe on the windowsill; bills and more bills. Once inside, he put a match to the wood-burner laid that morning, fixed himself a whisky and soda, and slumped into his armchair. He reached for the TV controls, switched to BBC1 and pressed the mute button. It was just before six o'clock. Through the windows, in the distance, the Eildon Hills rolled sensually.

His eyes were drawn towards the TV, his heart suddenly racing at the images; he fumbled with the controls to turn the volume up. There, quite clearly, grinning contempt at him in his sitting room were the faces of Sean Connor and Declan Murphy, the two men standing either side of some republican lawyer hailing the release of IRA prisoners as part of the Good Friday Agreement. Connor, in particular, wore a smug smile of victory about his broken features, his heavy-worn, open black leather jacket exposing a denim shirt and a crucifix. In a surreal parody to what he was witnessing, it was the cross around his neck, glinting in the afternoon sunlight, that filled his thoughts with the injustice of it all.

He had always known that this day would come, but had somehow denied it. He had known that it would goad him into violent feelings of retribution which he ought to suppress. Now they overwhelmed him. How could this terrorist gloat over killing one of his men in cold blood and get away with it? Piers grabbed his coat, slammed the door and strode off at a furious pace cross country towards the Eildon Hills.

Jenny was outside, clutching an armful of exercise books as she closed her car door. 'Piers, what on earth is wrong?'

'Nothing,' he growled. She knew better than to disturb him in one of his rare black moods.

Piers stomped up the grassy slope of the hill immediately behind his home, the oxygen in his lungs serving to assuage his fury. Dammit, wasn't he right to hate Connor and Murphy? Or was revenge like the pathetic satisfaction he'd hoped for in humiliating his tormentors at school? No, Connor and Murphy were the pathetic bullies. Normally society would shame and punish these men. But when there was no just law, shouldn't a guardian of society like a soldier, enforce it himself? That meant anarchy, vendettas and endless tribal feuds. Like Afghanistan, where everyone lived in fear, and life was so cheap that men with amputated limbs were two a penny; where life was so harsh that women of thirty looked like wizened crones of sixty – those that were visible of course.

He stopped in his tracks and looked down at the lush grassy bowl of the Teviot Valley, the security and tranquil beauty that he had known and loved since his childhood. He saw a mile away, a copse by a bend in the river where he had played Cowboys and Indians with his schoolboy friends, who still lived in the pebble-dashed bungalows in the village nearby. How exciting the idea of battle had seemed as a child, with the blissful certainty that you would somehow never get hurt – how different from the gruesome reality. Wasn't revenge just the same?

A little further to the left, the grey stone wall of his cottage glowed orange in the setting sun. A light was on in the sitting room; Jenny was waiting there, patiently correcting her pupil's clumsy attempts at French. This was where he belonged. He trudged back, deflated, apologised and explained his bad temper to her. He poured himself a whisky.

*

The metallic-blue Ford Mondeo drew into Cullyhana, past streetlights and the school railings decked with green, white and orange bunting. From the doorway of the Lite 'n Easy Pub a young man in working blue overalls had been looking anxiously up and down the street. On seeing the car turn the corner he rushed inside and within seconds folk were tumbling over themselves to scramble through the door. Above the melee, pints of foaming black and brown liquid spilled down extended arms. Animated faces looked in on the passengers. The doors opened, letting in loud applause, shouts and cheers from the men; they were all men.

'Well dey couldn'y keep us in forever, Sean,' said Declan, smiling, though clearly moved by their reception. He embraced his friend in the back of the car before stepping out. The cheers grew louder and the two men were scooped up and carried shoulder high – like sporting heroes – into the bar. Clutching outstretched hands, they grinned like idiots at every welcome, not hearing what was said or recognising a soul.

The familiar long wooden bar on the right-hand side was littered with an assortment of glassware left by the mob. Patrick Meigh, the proprietor, had timed his pints to perfection and as the two men were put down so a pint of Smithwicks and a pint of Guinness were thrust into their hands.

'Welcome home, lads. We've missed ya,' he said.

'Aye, I bet ya have so,' said Murphy, his upper lip covered in the head of his pint.

Though at the centre of the party, Murphy at once felt on the periphery, more observed than the life and soul of it, and inwardly he detached himself from it. In contrast, Connor was smiling and engaging in chitchat with those around him, clutching his pint in almost childish delight. Murphy looked around the bar. Was this what he had spent the last seven years in jail for? Were these people, these scruffy, poor farmers, all that he had given his life towards? And Maggie and his boys, bereft of a father all this time? Damn right they were. What was life without one's family and one's community, and what were they without freedom and ideals.

A large man in a russet pullover beneath a much-patched tweed coat squeezed himself next to Murphy at the bar. His ruddy cheeks glowed in the heady atmosphere of the confined space, and yellowing eyes moistened as he spoke:

'Welcome home, son.' Murphy broke from his trance and turned to face his father, his white hair immaculately combed.

'Oh, Pa!' he exclaimed, putting down his pint and hugging his father. 'Oh, Pa, I'm so sorry about mam; so, so sorry.'

'Tank you, son. She had bin hangin' on to see youse get out. But 'twas not to be.' He looked into his Guinness. 'Well now, you'll be havin' a lot to do now y're back; a lot o' catchin' up to do, but don't go forgettin' your ol' dad now will ya?' He smiled a loving smile, and Murphy hugged him again.

'Eh, Dec, der Man wants to 'ave a quick word with you an' Seany in de corner over dere,' said a voice breaking into the intimate moment. Murphy's father released his son's embrace, nodded approvingly and winked at him. Murphy followed the messenger through the crowd, Connor ahead of him still milking the plaudits.

At the rear of the pub there was a window with a long table beside it, at which a small coterie of the IRA's South Armagh Brigade were seated. A broad shouldered man of five foot nine, his face pulled long by a thickset jaw and heavy, puffing cheeks, leaving his mouth parted like a menacing pike, stood up as Connor approached. The man rubbed his purple, bulbous nose twice with his right index finger, and then pushed the same hand through his thinning head of grey hair. He leaned his gut across the table and smiled warmly at the two ex-convicts, extending both his hands.

'Welcome home, boys, welcome! Welcome.' He shook each vigorously by the hand, taking hold of their elbows as he did so.

'Ah, 'tis good to be back, Tam, so it is,' said Murphy with equal warmth.

'Aye, 'tis good to sees youse again, Tam,' said Connor, knocking back the last of his pint and looking into the empty glass.

'Patrick! Patrick! Two more pints for de boys now, and same agin all round here,' said the big man with a sweep of his hand around the table. 'Now den, make room, make room.' The hangers on made way, leaving Tam, Murphy and Connor with two silent, rustic-looking cohorts.

'Now den, boys, have youse all you need to be getting' on wi' for now?' he asked paternalistically.

'Aye, to be sure, Tam,' said Murphy.

'Dat is 'cept de whereabouts o' de bastard dat put us inside,' Connor interjected.

'Well now you know dat de dues have been paid. De boy's been made an example of...'

'I didn't mean tat stinkin' tout Fran O'Dowd. I meant de bastard,' he strongly emphasised the word, but was smiling nonetheless, 'de Brit bastard dat put us in de slammer.' He took a pull on his fresh pint.

'Oh you don't hang about, do you Seany,' laughed Tam.

'As I recall it – an' pretty well I do so – nieder did dey.' Again he supped on his pint, but fixed his gaze on the impassive blue eyes of Tam.

'Aye well, we know to be sure who's to be dealt with, but we don't want dis to become personal. Dat's not what we're about. We'll deal – you'll deal – with de matter all in good time.' His unflinching eyes finished the debate. Connor looked ruefully into his pint. It was enough that they knew who was responsible and that one day he would get his chance.

'Now den, boys,' said Tam, engaging them in more jovial terms, 'you're looking a little pasty, if I may say so. I'd say dose Brit prisons aint done your health no favours. Let Dr Tam here prescribe a little sunshine into your diets. I tink dat a little trip abroad wouldn't go amiss for yourselfs – or for the cause of Murther Ireland.'

Chapter 5

The valley was a magical place of stillness and vitality; it had given Walker a sense of perspective throughout life, and he always came here when in need of solace and refreshment. The hills that dominated the peaceful river scene rolled kindly away to the south, and then Rubers Law rose more starkly in the distance; dark, craggy and solemn against the grey skies. Behind him the ground was steep and angular and patches of mature conifers mingled with the granite cliffs. On top of the precipice above him rose Fatlips Folly, a solitary fortification and a reminder that the history of the area had not always been so idyllic. In this contrast of past and present, of nature with its beautiful sustenance and pointed teeth, Walker found a natural playground for his thoughts and character.

Rain drummed heavily on the stationary car. He flicked the windscreen wipers and peered hopefully through the foggy glass. A watery sky to the fore promised some respite, the late afternoon sun yellowing the grey canopy. In the rear-view mirror he saw the headlights of a car moving at speed along the narrow, windy lane. A whoosh of water splashed the side of his car as it passed. Impatient to make the most of what remained of the day and conditions he stepped outside, pulling the collar of his Barbour coat around his throat. He looked left and right, tilted his dun-coloured Chitrali cap and removed his fishing rod from the roof of his car.

With his head down he crossed the fifty yards of lush, saturated pasture to the riverbank. The rain intensified with a final burst and then eased, and the gentle noises of the river morphed with those of the storm. He watched as symmetric ripples of varying sizes were carried at pace across the clean black face of the stream, interrupted only by boils of water at the pool's tail, narrowing between submerged features. On the further bank the ripples were deeper and broader, formed from burgeoning drops of rain gathered on the low overhanging branches of the alder trees.

By the river's edge the bank had subsided to form a grassy shelf. Here he crouched, laid his rod against its lip and watched the water. An occasional smoker, he reached into his jacket for a cigarette to warm himself and to pass the time as he planned his attack. He had fished many times on more productive rivers, but it was the serendipity of the sport on this poorer relative that excited him. He knew the lies of the fish, the ground, the conditions, but then again they changed year on year, and as the stock of fish grew scarcer so the skill of the fisher had to increase.

The rain had stopped but still the skies were overcast. Birds began to make themselves heard on the far bank. Beside him a grey-wagtail bobbed and twittered on the wet rocks, insensible to his presence. In the tail of the upstream pool, emerging from the shelter of the tree line, five mallard drakes cruised out into an eddy, shaking droplets from their fine heads. All this you could see if you just sat and watched.

Walker checked his fly – a little Ally-shrimp double – and ran his forefinger and thumb along the length of the cast. Even at this height of water a small fly would do, as the water was clear. A deep bodied, perhaps ten-pound, silver salmon leapt out of the water opposite him. His heart jumped, anticipation surging through him. Carefully he raised himself and stalked along the river's edge, conscious that the river was in fact a window to the easily-spooked fish.

The head of the pool foamed and gushed too ferociously for a fly, but quickly the water fanned out like a bowtie and carried a fly perfectly. It was here that Walker began to cast; at first methodically, covering the water precisely, but then with guile and rhythm as he cast further and further, gathering perfection, deftly landing long casts over the deep, inviting lies. With every cast he moved two yards down stream, and in so doing joined himself to the water via the spit of shingle.

The force built up around his legs as he got deeper into the water and created a 'V' of fast flowing ripples downstream of him. The peaty water made his chest-waders look like yellowing ancient parchment. He loved the cool sensation of the water pushing against him and to see the rope mesh of the round net, strapped across his back, billow out into the stream; the small rock he had placed in it dancing to the changing currents. He felt to his left with his wading-stick, slid two paces, steadied himself and cast again. The water was to his waist now.

Piers gave an involuntary shudder, as if someone had walked over his grave. His skin prickled. He had the feeling that he was not alone; a feeling that had served him well in the past. He turned his head to scan the ground behind.

A slow tug on his fly-line, like a tentative knock, alerted his sensibilities back to the river. The white line tightened across the black water. The tip of his rod bent gently as he lifted the rod firmly but smoothly. He bared his clenched teeth in excitement as the adrenalin pumped around his body expelling any immediate concerns. The fish dived deeper, racing upstream, the line zinging out of his reel. He let the fish run on until the line slackened as it stopped midstream. He turned his shoulders to the point in the water where the line disappeared into the blackness. He raised his rod powerfully, embedding the barb into the fish's mouth.

A cock pheasant was disturbed noisily from his roost behind Piers' left shoulder. He turned suddenly, and at the precise moment that the salmon launched itself impressively from the river, like a bar of silver. Piers turned back and in so doing seemed to lose his footing, as though his feet had been kicked from beneath him in a judo throw. His chest waders filled with water. His bottom bounced twice along the river's bed. The light above him darkened as if a curtain had been drawn across it. Madly he clasped at amber bubbles trying to pull himself up. He sank deeper. He kicked hard as he hit the bottom, and as his head breached the surface his left side was pummelled into a semi-submerged granite boulder.

Gasping for air he was sucked down into the torrent of intoxicating bubbles and noise. He was swept along at pace and yet interminably slowly. The danger was as much from drowning, concussion or entrapment in a snare of rock in the depths. He tumbled like an acrobat. He fumbled for the quick release catch of his net, freed it, and by chance found himself at the surface again.

He lay on a shingle beach on his back in the green gloaming. He began to laugh; at first sheepishly and then out loud building up to a crescendo. He pawed at the shingle and tossed it into the air. He had survived the ignominy of drowning a fool's death. His ribs ached. His head echoed the noise of the water. Gingerly he raised himself and headed back along the bank.

By dint of good fortune he came across his rod, lapping against the shore. He stooped to pick it up and reeled in the line. He shivered, the cold and shock beginning to seep into his bones. The evening was drawing in fast and with it the temperature was dropping. He cursed as the line tightened, caught behind a rock or snagged on a root.

The line jerked and drew out, lighting up his senses like an electric shock: incredibly the salmon was still hooked. Calmly and with the greatest respect for his prey, Piers began to reel in the fish.

Above him the jet stream peeled back the clouds to reveal the first stars and a brilliant white moon disc. He closed the gate, his rod and fish in one hand as he turned to face his car across the road. As he did so, he was caught in the full beam of a car's headlights. He tried to shield his eyes. The car door opened. A big man got out, advanced and stopped in the middle of the road. His hands were deep inside the pockets of his trench coat, his frame silhouetted against the lights. He stopped, relaxed his hands and opened out his jacket. Walker raised his hand holding the salmon and his rod:

'You're just in time for supper.'

Chapter 6

Walker reclined in his armchair in front of the wood-burning stove bursting with heat. He was wrapped in a blanket, wearing a thick white fisherman's roll-neck jumper, an old pair of corduroy trousers, and his shooting stockings.

'Goodnight you two. Don't stay up all hours chatting,' said Jenny as she kissed him tenderly on the forehead. She turned to the other man and winked.

Aware that Piers was watching her, she turned in the doorway and smiled contentedly at him, her misty brown eyes beckoning him to join her. God she was beautiful, he thought; thick, bouncy auburn hair flowing over her shoulders, olive skin from mediterranean origins, a pretty little snub-nose, and a winning, lopsided smile that warranted immediate reciprocation.

Piers stared at the empty space she had left, wanting to throw off his blanket and join her. He was a lucky man to have found someone like her. She was even-tempered, kind, thoughtful, and yet she did not impinge herself on his lifestyle like a creeping plant attaching itself to a vibrant sapling. She was more of a lone and exotic flower, and yet in harmony with the rambling garden in which she found herself. In two years they had never talked about it, but she seemed to have instinctively grasped that to keep Walker was to lose him, and she respected that. She had her own life as the secondary school's French teacher; she had her own cottage on a neighbouring farm, but she also had her own schedule, and the time was fast approaching when she would return home to France.

Barry Ferguson sat opposite him, watching with amusement. 'Don't let me keep you up,' he grinned, before taking a gulp from his whisky tumbler. Goaded by this, Walker shot him a glance of mock protest, threw off his blanket and reached for the bottle of whisky.

'She's a cracking bit o' stuff, Piers.'

'Ya, I know, Barry, I know.'

'What's she doing up here with a scamp like you, eh?'

'Well she didn't come here for me if that's what you mean. She came to teach. These French, or some of them at least, have a romantic notion about Scotland, and she's one of 'em.' He drank some whisky. 'We just hit it off. She's bright, funny, pretty, and she let's me do my own thing. Doesn't want to own me like some women.'

'An' is she staying?' he proffered, sensing that there was a 'but' coming.

'Well...' Walker sighed deeply. 'She's due to go back next autumn. She has a job to take up at some university in Lyons.'

'An' you don't want her to go, eh,' he chuckled.

'There aren't many girls like her about, especially not up here. I mean there's Edinburgh, but they're city types. Couldn't hack a winter down here. Never thought that I'd settle down. But hell, it feels so natural. She really fits, if you know what I mean. But – and it's a big but – she won't hang about without any commitment from me.' He paused and shifted his gaze from Barry to the fire, growing reluctant to take the conversation any further. Seeing this, Ferguson changed the subject.

'So tell me what you've been doing with yourself – apart from learning to swim with the fish that is?'

'What? Since I left the Regiment?'

'Yeah. I mean why aren't you in the City with all your Rupert friends minting it up?'

'It's not my thing. This is where I belong. Where I grew up, where I was moulded if you like,' he added self deprecatingly, dropping his eyes from Ferguson to his tumbler.

'But you've no family of your own. You can't go hanging off the apron strings forever, you know.'

'My family, though, are the people from round here. Many of them are second or third generation tenants.'

'And the business? Ain't that some sort of silver spoon?' gibed Ferguson.

Walker paused, nervous at having to justify his birthright to his old platoon sergeant. 'OK, so I don't know too much about fashion or style you might say, but I like to think that I can put something into the business. It is after all the business that has sustained my family over nearly two centuries.'

'Surely it's going the way of all heavy industry – especially textiles – and that's east?'

'Exactly. And that is why the community needs to diversify. It needs to face up to realities, else the folk from these parts will drift away and we'll be left with a shell that people come to admire and coo over because it's a pretty part of the world with a quaint history.'

'Like Jenny?' Ferguson said with a smirk.

'Maybe. Communities survive on people, and people need industry to keep going. And an industry needs labour. It's a very simple self-serving wheel, and it's got to be kept turning else it will stop.' He paused, bored of the conversation.

He saw that Ferguson too had allowed his concentration to drift towards the fire; fires do that. And whisky. It seemed to Walker that Ferguson had not noticed the pause. He detected an edge to his old comrade's demeanour since Jenny had left them – not totally relaxed, and yet trying to be. It was only little things, like sipping too soon after a rejoinder in the conversational flow – trying to chase it on to create an opening. Not quite the measured man he knew of old. *Why was he here? Not for the chat surely – not his style.* He studied him for a moment over the rim of his tumbler before breaking the silence:

'And why exactly did you drop by, Barry?'

Ferguson ignored the question. 'Do you mind if I put some music on?'

'Lead on,' he said, pointing his glass at the CD player beside Ferguson. The *Adagio* from Dvorak's Symphony Number Nine softly intruded. Ferguson frowned.

'I want to explore the country a bit before I head for the Dales again and thought I'd look you up,' he said with a smile more like his old self. He paused, looking deeply into the fire again, and then with significant intent – but conveyed matter-of-factly – he asked, 'Didn't you kick around Central Asia for a bit before discovering these principles?'

'Yeah, I did. It seems like an age away now,' he began to smile. 'A friend of mine got involved with a mine clearance charity in Afghanistan. It sounded interesting. I only meant to stay a while, but the place sort of got under my skin.'

'So you even tried to save a whole country from itself before starting on your own community! Is there no end to your worthiness?' The *Adagio* grew louder.

'Hey, Baz, leave it alone will you, and turn the music down else you'll wake Jenny,' he parried with a good-humoured smile. 'Anyway, it was purely self-indulgent. It's the most beautiful country on God's earth, and it's been pickled in poverty and war for the preservation of anyone with an interest in the ways of that world. But not too many folk have been able to enjoy it of late.' He stopped to refill his glass. He liked to reminisce about these times. He felt a sense of purpose and achievement about the experience and was warming to the conversation again.

'Where did you spend your time?'

'I'll show you my map if you're interested, and my photograph albums.'

'You bet I am.'

Walker disappeared into his study and returned with a boxful of photographs, an album and a ragged map. Jenny was standing in the doorway opposite him, slightly bleary eyed, wearing his threadbare navy towelling dressing gown and grinning at him.

'You're a little drunk, I think – no?' she challenged with that wonderful smile of hers.

'Not at all. I'm just getting my Afghan album out for Barry.'

'I thought you were coming to bed soon?'

He leant across and kissed her on the cheek. 'In a moment, I promise. I won't be long.' Barry giggled enviously to himself as he listened to the banter of the two lovebirds.

'Don't let him bore you for too long,' she called round the door to Barry. 'And Piers, perhaps you could turn the music down for me please.'

'Yes my love,' he said and kissed her again, at the same time pushing her back into the bedroom and closing the door behind her.

'We'll be for it in the morning now. Anyway – here, pull a chair up to the table and bring your glass with you,' he said, laying out his paraphernalia on the kitchen table.

'You spent two years out there?'

'Nearly three actually. I ranged about between Kabul, Jebel-Saraj and Pul-i-Khumri, either side of the Hindu Kush. Fantastic climbing and walking out there; all unspoilt and parts rarely, if ever explored.' He spread out the map and indicated the place names with a calloused forefinger. 'You interested in the Ancient World?' Ferguson shook his head.

Ferguson drew him off his historical musings: 'You must have been fluent in the lingo by the time you left, and pretty *au fait* with the layout?'

'Yeah. I was – still am I suppose though there's no call for it here. And as far as the ground goes… I wouldn't say so… but then again there ain't been too many climbing expeditions there in the last two decades. Only a few western journalists who tagged along with the Muj in the eighties would know it as well, I guess.'

A log shifted in the wood-burner, leaving a comet-like shower of cinders percolating through the grate; hungry flames licked around the dry unexposed wood as it settled.

'Do you still keep in touch with any of the natives?' he asked, without looking up from his glass.

'Bashir. He was my climbing partner and guide. One of four sons of the curator of the Kabul Museum – or what's left of it. Brilliant mountaineer – like an ibex: knowledgeable and cultured with it. He and I exchange letters three to four times a year, by runner so to speak. And then there's Kamir.' Walker smiled broadly as he remembered his old friend.

Kamir was the part-anglicised, eldest son of Fazir Khan, head of the Ishmaeli enclave in Kayan in the Hindu Kush, north of Kabul. After the fall of President Najibullah in 1992, the country had degenerated into a free-for-all. His father had summoned him home from his secular exploits in a Birmingham fast food chain to take up the defence of the family lands and people.

Incongruous with his surroundings and position, he had failed to entirely divest himself of his former habits. His homes throbbed to the sound of rock music, and his televisions looped Jane Fonda fitness videos for his oft-stoned entourage of salivating Mongoloid hill men. He drank Jack Daniels and beer, a pleasure not forbidden by his sect. In spite of his decadence, indeed perhaps because of it, he received feudal loyalty from his people.

'He runs a little fiefdom up here in Kayan. They're an Ishmaeli sect. We always got on well with them – could sort of relate to one another, but more so after I saved his life.' He paused to pick out Kayan on the map for Ferguson.

'Go on.'

'Nothing to tell really…pulled him from an RTA that took his cab into a minefield. Anyway, Kamir, the sentimental bugger, says I saved his life and swore he'd be forever in my debt. Thankfully he didn't have the chance to pay me back. But every Christmas I get a ragged parcel delivered by some dodgy Asiatic courier service. Bloody carpets!' he said with a mocking sweep of his hand around the room.

'And how did you get on with the Taliban?'

'Oh, they're all right really. They may seem a little peculiar to you and I when seeing them through our own prejudices. But I like to think of them enacting some kind of Reformation – mullahs in codpieces.' He paused, staring into the fire, before adding, 'It's not for us to determine how the world should live… and yet it is in a funny sort of way. That is what they're doing after all – interpreting a way of life.'

'Well I guess that's not a view you read in the Guardian. But how do you square that with them hosting some of the nastiest forms of terrorist in the Islamic world?'

'It won't last. They'll realise that they need the West to survive and will accommodate them by removing – if they have the power to do so – the nexus of terrorism. It's not just about political will. Look at our own little problem in Ulster.' Conscious that he was getting over-excited by his pitch for the Taliban to a none-too-enthusiastic audience, he paused to drink off his whisky tumbler. 'Anyway, enough of my ranting; you didn't really tell me what brought you up here, did you? I don't have you down for a social drop-in.'

Ferguson didn't meet his eyes. He looked down into the glass, twiddling it in his hands like a goalkeeper turning a ball before punting it up field.

'How did you feel about Murphy and Connor being released?'

Walker laughed sardonically and refilled his glass, the raw emotions of the past weeks beginning to well up inside him again. No one could fully appreciate how it felt to see the things that you'd given your life to, turned upside down. The murderers you'd risked your life to put away, released for no evident gain. Only Ferguson would know. Only Ferguson would be thinking what he thought but could never articulate, let alone enact. *'At last we cut to the chase,'* he thought. He passed the bottle to Ferguson. 'So you had the same call I take it?'

'Er... I don't know what you mean – what call?' Walker noticed that Ferguson seemed to falter. Why hadn't he got a call? They'd been to the same bloody trial hadn't they, and what's more, given evidence.

'What! I don't believe it! How could they not give you the same pathetic spiel they gave me?' He leant forward, elbows on his knees and staring into Ferguson's eyes.

'Like I said, I've been on the road these last few weeks mooching about and chasing old flames from my little black book,' he said with a grin, but now with a more inquisitive look, his square head cocked to one side.

'Some fucking,' he emphasised the word strongly, though he had no need to as he rarely swore, 'pen-pusher from the MoD rang to offer me advice about the release of Connor and Murphy. Can you fucking believe it?'

'They did what? What do you mean?'

'I tell you what I mean: first they offered me some sort of counselling lest the release brought back some bad memories.' He shook his head in disbelief at his own words. 'And then this sort of quasi-victim-support-unit asked me if I knew the drill on seeing anything suspicious. And to cap it all they ended their piece by stating baldly that *'revenge isn't PIRA's bag – well not unless practised on their own kind'* – this last the shyster uttered with a smug little laugh.' Ferguson nodded his head slightly, encouraging Walker to go on. 'I told the little fuckwit, who's probably seen nothing more dangerous than a champagne cork fly through the air at Royal Ascot, that perhaps if his people didn't go letting these bastards – who deserved everything they got by the way – out of jail then we wouldn't be having this conversation.'

'And he said?'

'I slammed the phone down and didn't let him come back.'

'A pity I missed that call.' He turned his glass in his hands. 'He's got a point though.'

'And that would be?'

'Well... I mean... they don't practice revenge on the likes of us – do they?'

'Why wait to find out.' His eyes had a fixed glaze about them boring straight through Ferguson. 'I mean, why not take them out – if the government won't, why shouldn't we?'

'Because you'd never get away with it. And because you're better than that – better than them. You'd be taking yourself to their level if you did that. Besides, you'd end up exactly where they should be: banged to rights,' said the old platoon sergeant calmingly. 'And let's not forget that solid background of yours – wouldn't that get in the way, eh?'

Walker was angry – very angry. Emotions repressed even from his subconscious – repressed by his upbringing – had been tapped and exposed beyond those which had surfaced on seeing the news some weeks ago. Why should he feel wrapped in the straightjacket of conformity? Ferguson not only was pointing this out, but in so doing also tightening the straps. Hell, if the IRA can get away with it because they play by no rules that conform to his own, why should he play by the rules? Corporal Hill wasn't the only one that they'd killed; and there'd be more somewhere down the line too.

'But then again, what if you could get away with it, eh, Barry? I mean: you know people – I know people – we know people. It could be done. They're laughing at us, Barry – laughing at me, here in my sitting-room, here in the Borders. Smirking out of my bloody TV set.'

Ferguson broke the trance-like engagement of eyes and looked into the fire. He changed the subject:

'Would you ever go back to Afghanistan?'

Walker laughed, and threw his head back. 'I don't think it's on Jenny's top ten list of most desirable holiday destinations, if you get my drift.'

'Just before I left the Regiment I discovered an interesting thing.' He swung forward, and looked intently at Walker. 'The IRA are exploring links with Osama bin Laden's al-Qa'eda group.' He smiled as Walker looked incredulously at him. *How could an Islamic fundamentalist terrorist organisation possibly get into bed with a secular group like the IRA?*

'Don't look so surprised. You know as well as anyone about their Middle Eastern links with Libya and the PLO in the past. Lately they've got involved with the Columbian Farq group. An' then there's the Eastern Europeans. They're an unscrupulous bunch of hoods – you know that.'

'OK, but there's a world of difference between the fundamentalist Islamics and a wholly secular crew like the IRA. It doesn't add up,' he said, feeling his anger cool with the change of tack.

'It's straightforward really. Paddy wants weapons, drugs, 'n a safe place to train away from the spotlight. Bin Laden's organisation wants to create as much terror in the West that they can. Now of course they want to create that terror, but if they can use an effective organisation to tie up western resources – political, military and economic – then why not use a proxy? It's like a symbiotic relationship: ideologically they're diametrically opposed, and yet they feed off each other. Paddy doesn't believe that the mullahs have a hope in hell of winning, and the mullahs don't feel threatened by the 'local' Irish conflict. A perfect odd couple relationship, but its success relies on total secrecy. Al-Qa'eda would lose respect from other fundamentalists. And PIRA is playing a dangerous game too, when with the other hand it's brokering a peace deal. But they haven't really renounced their struggle.'

'And yet,' said Walker, warming to the concept, 'al-Qa'eda operatives have in the past coloured themselves with Western culture in order to blend in. If they're caught they'll justify it with "Hell! Why not...?" and as you say, the IRA are completely unscrupulous.'

The two men sat staring across the table at the walls as though exhausted by a mental exercise.

'And?' said Walker, excitement churning inside.

A reflected twist of flame caught in the near empty whisky bottle between them.

Walker stood in the doorway of his bedroom, looking at Jenny as she slept soundly; her serene, beautiful face turned towards him and her bare left arm draped across the pillow. The cream strap of her short silk slip hung off her shoulder; a slip that would have invitingly ridden up to the small of her back, revealing her warm smooth bottom. Whisky and sexual desire tingled in his brain. He stripped off and slinked between the sheets, turned out the light and cuddled up behind her, their bodies entwining perfectly. He put his left arm across her side, and rested his hand on the silky indent of her waist. She stirred and pulled his arm tightly across her, slipping his hand beneath the strap and clasping it to her soft breast.

'You smell of whisky,' she muttered.

He tenderly nuzzled her ear, and felt her body react with goose pimples. She giggled and arched her head towards him like a playful cat. 'You're late,' she toyed. 'What kept you?'

'Oh, nothing. Just catching up.'

'He's come a long way to catch up. And a surprise visit?'

'Yeah – but we go back a long way.' She could tell Walker wasn't interested in talking, but she sensed that there was more to it. She liked Barry, but detected in him a strong, silent desire and a scheme that involved Piers. She knew little of Piers' past before leaving the army; it was a closed book between them that she wouldn't open. She did know about the ambush in South Armagh – Piers had explained what had gone on that night he had stomped off into the hills. Was it too much of a coincidence that Ferguson should appear now, for the first time in the two years she had known him?

'What did he want you to do?' she asked coyly, pulling him tighter towards her.

'Me? Oh, nothing. He had some mad plan that he wanted me to join him with.'

She was silent, scared that she might lose him. He had been a man of action. Could he really find contentment and satisfaction in the quiet of a Borders life and in marriage – which was her dearest wish? 'You won't go with him, will you, Piers?' She pleaded sweetly into the pillow. She had a dreadful feeling of an impending and abrupt finality.

But to Walker, her words sounded like a challenge that pricked him. He perceived the rattle of chains where there were none. 'Of course not,' he lied and pulled her round towards his face.

*

The following morning was cold and drizzly as Ferguson pulled his blue Vauxhall Vectra up outside the Ancrum Village Post Office. An old fashioned red public telephone box, the nearest to Walker's house, stood beneath the receding canopy of a huge walnut tree. Puffs of black coal-smoke belched from the chimneys of the twee stone-fronted houses flanking the triangular village green. An elderly man, wearing a brown tweed coat and grey-blue flat cap shuffled past him, pursued by an overweight fluffy collie dog. The man stopped to talk to a middle-aged woman half his size, carrying a bag of groceries from the shop. He raised his cap and shuffled on.

Ferguson smiled as he took in the chocolate-box scene of ancient manners. He got out of his car and entered what could possibly be the cleanest phone box in Britain. He dialled a number from memory, a fifty pence piece engaged in the slot.

'Hello,' answered a brusque but well-educated male voice at the other end. He rammed the coin home and the beeping stopped.

'Ferguson here.' His breath condensed on the black mouthpiece.

'Speak.'

'He's taken it. He'll make the necessary arrangements. We're gonna meet up in the smoke in a week's time.'

'Good work. Keep me posted on your movements.'

'Will do. Cheerio then.' He replaced the receiver.

Dressed in a Savile Row chalk-stripe flannel suit, the man sat back in his chair and looked out of his office window. He pushed his hands across his scalp, his ginger hair held neatly in position by D.R. Harris of St James Florimel hair oil.

The telephone call had excited him keenly, but his attention rested lazily on the slow rotation of the Millenium Wheel across the river before returning to the black briefcase embossed with the royal cipher.

Chapter 7

Summer 2001 – Pakistan

Sean Connor and Declan Murphy were met at Islamabad by their ISI contacts, and two days later found themselves in an olive-green Land Cruiser speeding westwards along the dusty tarmac road heading out of Peshawar.

Seen through a chimera of heat and tinted windows they passed displays of weaponry from Peshawar's arms bazaar. The two clean-shaven white faces gawped like children in a sweet shop. In the front, their non-conversational Taliban driver stared straight ahead; more concerned that one of the stream of pedestrians flanking the road might stray into their path. His superiors had left him in no doubt that his passengers were too important for any mishaps.

The turbans of the driver and his solitary escort were tied neatly like old-fashioned liquorice toffee wrappings. They fitted tightly over broody aquiline features, leaving a shoulder length tail that lifted with every jolt of the pock-marked road. Black eyebrows and bushy beards sprouted from their faces like horsehair stuffing from a dilapidated armchair. Coal-black eyes showed no signs of humour, nor perhaps humanity, to the Irishmen.

'I bet deir blood runs black,' said Sean Connor beneath his breath. The Taliban in the passenger's seat turned his head and screwed his eyes menacingly, his hands resting on the careworn wooden stock of the AK47 rifle between his legs. 'Jeez, I didn't tink dey could understand fockin English.'

'Det can't. Just relax and enjoy de ride will you,' smiled Murphy.

'How can I enjoy de fockin ride when I know dat I'm gonna be spendin' de next two months in a place totally alien to me. And,' here he animated his voice with heavy sarcasm, 'what's more, a place dat's as dry as a nun's fanny. I ask ya!'

'Still, tink of de cause, Seany, eh? Tink of it as an adventure. Or would ya rather still be languishing in de slammer, eh?'

'Aye, to be sure, y're right, Dec. Why should a man be gloomy?'

The arid plains on either side gradually gave way to steep prophetic foothills, proclaiming in the distance the massive grey Safed Mountain Range delineating the Afghan border. The ground was ruffled and pulled up to them like an unmade bed, through which the Land Cruiser moved effortlessly like a steam iron. Hilltop forts speckled the immediate horizons. By the roadside, in an almost atavistic impulse of the British Raj, whitewashed boulders lay tidily arranged. The road snaked its way between steep mountain flanks in parallel with the railway line. Connor's mind's eye had painted a tableau of pith-helmeted red coats stood-to along the ramparts of these adobe forts, only to be picked off by Afghan jezails fired unseen from behind every boulder. He smiled:

'De Khyber focken' Pass! Scene of British defeat 'n blood! Don't de air smell sweet still, eh, Dec? What was it: 1842 and de whole bloody army retreated in tatters, butchered to de one last solitary doctor. An' den dey had de audacity to tink tat dey could stick deir noses in de trough again a second time. Well dose cut-troats seen to dem alright.'

'Your memory is selective. Dere were some brave people – on all sides.'

'Of course,' said Connor sarcastically, 'I was forgettin' de "glorious" Murphy heritage of levering de pot-bellied Brits onto deir imperial podium.'

'He was press-ganged,' retorted Murphy with mock tetchiness. 'He just happened to be rather good at it, dat's all.'

'I bet he was,' said Connor, rubbing his nose as if trying to get rid of a bad smell.

'My great-great-uncle—'

'Notin' too great about him if you ask me.'

'He was requisitioned into de Bengal Horse Artillery from de navvies, and den joined de Corps of Guides – a sort of latter day SAS if you like. Decorated an' all sorts he was. He had quite a hand at dat insurgency stuff; spying out de land, and de enemy and reporting back.' This last he uttered with something approaching pride, which Connor detected and scorned.

'You'll be claiming next dat de bloodline of heroism runs true in your veins – Brit heroism and collusion dat is!'

'Well Seany, ya can't knock a brave man whatever his motives may be. He was one of the last to fall beside Lieutenant Walter Hamilton VC when dey slaughtered de Brit Politicals in Kabul. Der's a statue of 'im in de old Dublin museum.'

'Oo' your Uncle Billy?'

'Na, ya oaf – Hamilton. Seventy men held out all day, mostly natives, against swarms of Afghans before the last man fell.'

'Died a hero, did he? A Brit hero?'

'Aye, he did dat. Dey butchered him on de spot; put his head on a spike an' paraded 'im round de city. Heathen bastards.' He looked nervously at the implacable faces of their escorts. 'A little plaque in some God-forsaken hole called Mardan commemorates deir sordid little deed of heroism. For what?'

'An' how de wheel turns, eh Dec. Uncle Billy's boy is about to enter de catacomb of imperial folly on an entirely different mission, wearing de different colours now. Perhaps he'll have a chance to cleanse de Murphy honour of de stain of an infamous blackguard of a forebear. Eh, Dec?'

But Murphy wasn't listening, his attention was drawn through the windscreen to the blue painted double iron gates, and a little wooden hut beneath the shady awning of an ancient mulberry tree in fruit.

Beside the hut two Pakistani border guards sat behind a school desk with piles of paper weighed down with rocks, and flanked by two moustached soldiers with machine guns strapped across their chests. In front of them stood an orderly queue of hirsute Asiatics in pyjama suits, and women covered from head to toe in pastel coloured chaderis.

'De Towr Khan Gates, Seany. You'd best keep your opinions to yoursel' from now on. Tings ain't changed much in dis neck o' de woods since Uncle Billy's days.'

The driver lifted his hand in recognition to the guards, who in return signalled to the soldiers by the gates as though brushing away a persistent fly. The black bereted guard pulled back the rudimentary bolt, whilst his compatriot barred the way of the immediately evident and unruly mob on the other side. The driver waved again, and drove on. He honked his horn as the Afghan crowds slowly parted. His companion raised himself in his seat to look above them, muttered something unintelligible to his passengers and eased back.

Beyond the melee was a matching Land Cruiser, parked on the serrated edge of the tarmac road in front of the wooden shack that served as the Afghan passport office. The passenger door opened on seeing the other emerge. A tall, willowy man in an immaculate white pyjama suit got out, wearing an equally pristine white cotton turban, like a meringue on top of his head. He had long black eyelashes, a good deal of hooked nose, and a bushy black beard overhanging his pointed, jutting jaw. From the side his whole visage looked like a miniature set of stairs leading up to two twinkling brown eyes that drew one in with warmth and cunning, like a fox. He stood on the roadside waiting for the Irishmen. Long, thin fingers entwined in front of his crotch, pointing down to a dusty and incongruous pair of black military combat boots. He was an image of paradox; the sybaritic slyness of the Oriental combined with the ruggedness of a fighting man.

Beside him, but set back from the roadside, an audience of three Afghans squatted beneath a mulberry tree. Dressed in altogether more prosaic garb of brown and olive pyjamas and grey worsted waistcoats, they masticated gloomily as they stared through the advancing Land Cruiser towards the disappearing Khyber Pass.

The man in white walked towards the Land Cruiser, as Connor and Murphy emerged, blinking into the dazzling sunshine. The 45 °C of dry heat hit them like a wall after their air-conditioned ride. He raised his arms to greet them, his teeth smiling like a toothpaste advertisement against the backdrop of black whiskers.

'Welcome to Afghanistan, gentlemen,' he gushed, grabbing each in a double-handed handshake. 'My name is Abdul Qadir.'

*

A couple of days later, a tall, broad-shouldered traveller strolled aimlessly past Green's Hotel in Peshawar. Little taxis with two-stroke engines and horse-tail tassels of glitter buzzed up and down the otherwise languid Sadder Road in the stifling noon heat. His bleached hair unwashed in weeks was tied back in a ponytail. An unkempt ginger beard curled, from much stroking, underneath his prominent chin. Around his neck he wore an amulet on a leather thong, which nestled in a rug of sweaty chest hair revealed beneath an open necked, collarless cotton shirt. Cool, beige pantaloons extended to size twelve, open-sandalled grubby feet. On his right shoulder hung a sun-faded canvas knapsack.

For two consecutive days Barry Ferguson had taken this prescribed route, expectant of the rendezvous. And each day he had returned to his hostel to live among the squalor of flies and two leftover hippies immersed in the local garb and hash. He had operated solo before, but always with backup. This time it was different, and he felt the isolation in this alien environment. They knew that Connor and Murphy had entered the country and by now would have made contact with their handlers and probably be across the border; having good friends in intelligence had been of immeasurable help. Now it was entirely up them to close down their quarry. He almost envied the Irishmen as he thought of the arduous entry that he and Walker must make on foot to enter Afghanistan unseen.

A small, wall-eyed boy sat outside a shop on a pile of jute sacks, warming a billycan of chai over a sparking brazier. 'You want change dollars, mister?' he said, showing his yellowing teeth.

Ferguson looked at the boy, who nodded, and entered the spartan, dimly lit emporium. The boy ushered him silently to a rickety set of wooden stairs and motioned that he should go up.

At the top of the stairs there was a single room looking across the street, with a waxy muslin blind drawn across the open window. A deep, black and red Afghan carpet expansively filled the room, with similar patterned cushions lining the three walls. In the centre, two half-drunk glasses of muddy chai stood on the floor, behind which two Asiatic gentlemen sat cross-legged, contentedly sharing a hookah. Ferguson eyed them suspiciously.

Both had long, well-groomed black beards, and were dressed in unspectacular brown pantaloons and pyjama shirts, with high-collared, Nehru-style, grey worsted waistcoats. The smaller of the two wore no headdress and his face was discernibly that of a Pathan, the region's dominant race: deep eye sockets, with heavy black eyebrows shrouding nut-brown eyes; his lank hair was of a similar nut-brown colouring; he had a long face buoyed by his full beard and an aquiline nose, and his complexion, common to the Pathan, was an unexpected rosy white.

His companion was of an altogether firmer stature, perhaps taller, but noticeably more sinewy, evident in the strong hands and wrists exposed when passed the hookah to smoke. On his head he wore a khaki linen turban, into which was tucked most of his brown hair. From his face it was plain that he was not a Pathan. His complexion was darker, and his eyes singularly green, his nose flabby and not protrusive. The two men observed their intruder like a pair of owls whose vigil was being encroached upon.

'Welcome to our humble abode, Barry,' said Piers Walker, with a theatrical bow as he removed his headdress and smiling broadly. 'This is Bashir, of whom you know as much as I.' Bashir bowed his head politely to Ferguson and resumed his pipe. 'Now Barry, how the devil are we to pass you off as a native? You're a good bit taller than your average Afghan. Fancy losing a couple of inches, eh?'

'You utter bastard!' expostulated Ferguson, paying no heed to his jest. 'I've been wandering round this shitehole like some gormless hippy for two days waiting for your little elf-like creature to pop up. You been havin' a jolly good laugh 'ave you?'

'I am sorry, Barry, but Bashir had a couple of hiccups with the plan to move us up country. It couldn't be helped. Put it down to cultural experience.' He looked his old comrade up and down, tutting to himself. 'What do you reckon, Bashir? A haircut – a wash would be nice for all of our sakes – some walnut dye all over. The beard'll do. We'll need to sort the hair colouring out. A suit of pyjamas, and we'll pass him off as some form of half-breed, do you think?'

'There are some like him all over Afghanistan, since the Russian occupation especially, but also from before with the traders. I'm sure that we'll cope – so long as he doesn't speak.' He resumed his solemn smoke.

'Good point. How did you get on with the phrase book and tapes that I sent you?'

'*Salaam alekom. Hobesti – Hobestam. Ma name est Fareed.*'

Bashir choked, bubbling his hubbly-bubbly. 'Not bad, Mister Barry, but the accent, well it's kind of funny.'

Ferguson leant across to Walker. 'What's he mean by the 'Mister'? Does 'e think I'm one of your Rupert friends? An' what's so funny about my accent?'

'Relax. It's just their way. If you don't like the 'Mister' ask him to call you Barry. But from the moment you leave this shop you're going to become a mute. Bashir's right, you may pass for a hybrid by appearance but not by dialect. The language is for emergencies only. It is absolutely imperative that we infiltrate without being compromised by the Taliban or their agents. The whole town, the whole frontier, and much of the area we're to move in is Taliban controlled. It's the one chance we've got to slip in and out without anyone ever knowing we've been here.'

*

Tall flickering flames flirted vigorously with the sparks shot up from the crackling campfire, chasing them into a cocoon of smoke that embraced and choked them. Wafted by the heat, and then caught by the breeze, the smoke drifted over the congenial gathering of the caravan, half of which were engrossed in tall tales, hot-stew and merriment; the other in child-like trances in this centuries-old scene at the end of a weary day's march. They stared wondrously at the poplar leaves, reflecting the honeyed hue of the fire and shimmering in the breeze like a belly dancer's mirror-disked skirt. Above them the whippy trees swayed gently, tantalising the watchers below with glimpses of a silvery full moon.

Camels were masticating contentedly behind the party with their tent-like panniers lying beside them. The encampment was placed a hundred yards from the track, and double that distance from the river. The track linked Durband and Dung Gushten from east to west, whilst the river meandered its way towards the Arkari Gol River, linking eventually with the Chitral. Dung Gushten, an insalubrious settlement – though charming perhaps in its authenticity – lay on the edge of the porous Pakistan-Afghan border. The powindahs – nomads – have traversed the border regions for centuries, but less so since the Soviet occupation. The routes remain open for gun and drug running, as well as for more legitimate forms of trade. Bashir, though not a native of the region, had been given a verbal reconnaissance of the most expeditious route for their clandestine purposes.

He sat cross-legged beside his brother-in-law, Rassoul, a sagacious looking Bajauri with a grey rooted beard dignified by a shocking tinge of red hena on its extremities. His cheeks were pinched and his face lined and weathered by the road. Wrapped in a grey woollen shawl he quietly munched through his goat kebab supper, happy to let the reverie of his younger companions continue without the benefit of his opinions. Bashir leant across him, placed two hands around Rassoul's extended right hand and kissed him fondly on both cheeks whilst each muttered familiar farewells. He stood up, and without a word or a glance, Ferguson and Walker followed him into the night, each with an AK-47 and a small knapsack slung over their shoulders.

*

The Britons' heads began to pound as the air became thinner and colder from four to five thousand metres. Though both men were used to high altitudes it was nonetheless hard going and monotonous, with each reliant upon watching the footfalls of Bashir and the other. It had been like walking though a grainy black and white photograph, the landscape lit up by the ebbing moon. The early stages had been accompanied by the piping of cicadas as they brushed through thorny acacias on the plain. The backdrop of camp chatter and the tinkling of the river grew ever fainter. Now only the sound of their thudding hearts and heavy breathing filled their ears.

They had been climbing for nearly three hours when Bashir stopped abruptly and turned to Walker.

'We're being followed,' he said without emotion.

Ferguson caught up with the pair, his breath mirroring the efforts of his lungs in the moonlight. 'What's the hold up?' he whispered.

'Bashir reckons we're being tailed.' Ferguson looked behind him into the darkness, and strained his ears. He heard nothing.

'There may be nothing to it – an old man making a start to collect sticks.'

'At this time?' said Ferguson. 'I can't hear anything.'

'He's been with us for some time. When we passed the village, you heard the dogs?'

'Yeah but so what? People live there.'

'Exactly, and the dogs were startled. And before we stopped I heard a small landslide – just a few tumbling rocks. He's still some way off, but he is with us.'

Ferguson looked at Piers in the half-light. 'What do we do now?'

'We'll set up a snap ambush and see who he is. No shooting. It can't be anyone from the caravan – can it Bashir?' he asked.

'I don't know. I don't know the people of the caravan, only Rassoul.'

The three men found some cover just off a sharp turn in the track and waited, shivering as the sweat cooled on their backs.

They did not have to wait long. They heard the lazy stride of the man tripping occasionally on the track, knocking rock on rock. Bashir picked him out from his lolling gait. He was a young man of no more than twenty, wrapped tightly against the cold. His head was covered with his shawl, like an old woman. He had been the tea-boy in the caravan. He was called Noor. No more than a sapling amongst the men.

Ferguson had recognised him too. As soon as the boy turned away from him, he pounced, throwing him to the ground. He locked his arm behind him in a half nelson, and with his right arm held him tight about the throat. The Afghan was choking, his eyes bulging from their sockets.

'Leave him be,' said Walker in English, and immediately cursed himself. Ferguson relaxed his grip.

'Noor, isn't it?' Walker asked the youth in Dari. He nodded his head in the affirmative, unable to speak through fear and physical impediment. 'Why are you following us?'

The boy was terrified. It was dark and was freezing. His arm hurt like hell. His head was throbbing with the altitude. He had only once before been this high. He had never been physically attacked before. 'My uncle,' he stammered, 'my uncle… he lives over the pass. He lives in Bashgal. I have to give him news of his brother… my father… he is dying.'

'At this time of night?' The boy looked meekly at Walker as if to say, '*Well you are aren't you*?'

Bashir stepped forward. 'Bashgal is down the valley on the other side.'

'Do you know the way?'

'I've been this way only once before. Many years ago, when I was a boy… when we left Afghanistan.' He looked down at his feet, his toes protruding through rubber sandals.

'Well you'd better tag along with us for the night then, Noor,' said Walker, adjusting the boy's shawl for him. In the dark Ferguson scowled at Piers.

Bashir scampered as effortlessly as an ibex across the rough ground of the little-used powindah track. They stopped to rest before the snowline and looked down into the valley, picking out the serpentine progress of the river reflecting the silvery thread of the approaching day.

'The path goes over the pass. Maybe an hour – maybe two. We must break from it here. There's another path that the old men use for their wood. It'll take us to the northern peak of the pass, and into the snow. *Insha'Allah* we will be there by dawn.'

The sky paled first to a drab green, discarding all but the brightest stars, and then lightening into an ever more encouraging blue. Their journey had technically been nothing more than a walk at altitude, although at times it necessitated clambering over scree-slopes on all fours. Now, as Bashir pointed to the summit two hundred metres above them – on what appeared a gentle incline – it developed into a one-man race.

At last freed from the blindness of the night and Bashir's instinct, Ferguson forged on ahead like a man unshackled from a chain gang. He left the semi-discernable path and scrambled his way straight up, darting between all forms of obstacle. Had Walker not known him so well he may have feared that he was showing the first signs of hypothermia.

Ferguson placed one hand behind a fixed piece of rock and heaved himself up. His eyes drew level with ten bare toes in open sandals. Between the two feet rested the wooden butt of an AK-47. He followed the rifle up. It disappeared into a snow- and ice-crusted shawl wrapped around the body of a middle-aged Afghan. He was wearing only the indigenous lightweight garb. Ferguson tightened every muscle in his body. The man squatted precariously on the ledge, sheltered from the icy wind. His black beard was frosted over, and his eyes had a cold, melancholic stare – a stare as cold as death itself. From his nose a stalactite had begun to form.

Joining the race, Bashir had nimbly cut across the track and in two tacks had leapfrogged above Ferguson to the top. He looked down at him, startling the ex-soldier further. He proffered his hand, and pulled him round the frozen sentinel, whose ghoulish stare seemed to pursue him. Bashir laughed, 'Welcome to Afghanistan, my friend. Life is fragile is it not?'

MAP OF AFGHANISTAN

Chapter 8

They sat on top of a snow-dusted crest, huddled in their shawls, their caps and turbans pulled tightly down against the buffeting north-east wind. Above the Chitrali Hills, and behind them, the sun rose, warming swathes of ground like a laser beam. Their frigid eerie was as yet untouched by its warmth. In the half-light they nibbled naan bread, sipped from their water bottles and drank in the beauty of all that they surveyed, feeling well pleased with their progress. Walker and Ferguson felt more like pre-dawn Munro-baggers in the Scottish Highlands than infiltrators of a nefarious land.

'We did better than muckerjee back there,' grunted Ferguson. 'Thought you said no-one ever came this way, Bash?'

'Who knows who he was. A smuggler's lookout? Someone on the run? It makes no difference to him now.' Bashir stared wistfully into the bowl of the Bashgal Valley and beyond the death of this solitary man. 'It doesn't pay to sit around too long.' Noor gave a terror stricken glance over his shoulder towards the corpse and hugged himself to keep out the cold.

Now, for the first time sitting on the Afghan-Pakistan border and on the precipice of their hare-brained, unsupported mission, Walker pondered on what lay ahead with clarity and focus. It had been the same when he had taken the job with the mine clearance charity – impulsive, and quickly on the ground with little time to think about his motivations. He'd joined the army because that was expected of him; he'd joined the SAS because he was driven: young, idealistic and in search of adventure. When he'd left the army he'd felt the need to add a cause to his shopping list, before embarking on his sedentary family quest back home.

Now, here he was again – searching, chasing the inner demons that taunted him. But this time it was different; there was definition. The cause was personal.

'While we're sitting around up here, Bashir' said Walker, shaking himself from his wandering thoughts, 'we might as well sketch out the next phase.'

Below them the Bashgal River arced its way from its headwaters, a barely discernible puddle, where an amalgam of shepherds' huts, unseen by them, lay at the junction with the river. 'Looks like a sperm,' muttered Ferguson. On the other side of the bowl, and leading into the Bashgal's headwaters, the Suigal River cut a wound through the shiny ice and snow flecked fabric of the Kebrek Hills, more than six thousand metres above sea-level at their peaks, and twenty miles from them as the crow flew. The Semenek Pass was below them.

'That's Paniger at the bottom, by the lake,' Bashir indicated toward the unseen huts. 'We'll head down there. They know me from previous ferangi expeditions way back when the Shuravi were here; I took some journalists into the Panjsher. We'll get more supplies if we can, and then over the Dogu.'

'And how long will that take?'

'Two days. Maybe less. It will be the first test of your acting skills.' He smiled at Ferguson. 'You see the Dogu-da – at the shoulder of the snowline?' He pointed vaguely across the void, drawing his finger along the hilltops to the north. Beneath the incisor-like jaws of the Kebrek peaks, shadowy arêtes, like sinews, wove their way to the tops.

'That's the pass. It's just a walk. Then we'll follow the Tshocka Valley down on the other side into the Borish. And then it's onto the Anjoman easily in one day. Somewhere there we'll pick up my cousin Safiola's caravan for the Khawak Pass. Then we go into the Andarab. A week's march – maybe two.'

'As easy as that, eh?' grumbled Ferguson.

'And over there,' said Bashir, engaging Noor with a kindly smile as he pointed along the Bashgal, 'around the corner – you see? That's the track towards your uncle.' Noor followed the path traced for him with a mournful and half-witted gaze; he said nothing. His senses seemed numbed by the night's exercise at such altitudes; the only feeling that he had was that of being a passenger, and for that he was grateful.

Four pairs of eyes fixed on a single speck in the open sky. A golden eagle quartered the green pastures of the corrie below them, the tips of its wings turned up as it drifted with the wind. Walker put his binoculars onto the bird. Its neck was craned and its wings seemed to flutter effortlessly to hold its position. Then it dived. He followed the steep descent, losing it through the perpendicular edifices. Bashir shivered and packed away his water bottle, his eyes filled with moisture.

Like a stalker on a scottish hill, Bashir saw it first, pointing out to at least one interested party the solitary brown dipper hopping in and out of the more violent progress of the stream below them.

'Very pretty,' mocked Ferguson, picking beneath his big toenail with a twig.

Then it happened. No one had paid the boy much attention. That was the problem. His head had been drooped between his legs whilst they rested. Now he raised it. It was ashen. His eyes were delirious: dilated and cloudy. His lips were pale. He projectile vomited between his legs. He retched again. He stood up. His legs gave way beneath him. He was gasping for air.

'Mountain sickness,' said Walker urgently in Dari to Bashir. Ferguson knew without understanding what had been said. Secretly he felt pleased. The boy was a threat. He would slow them down; he could even compromise them – and they hadn't even got going. Better to let him die unseen and unmourned for. But he hadn't reckoned on Captain Compassionate.

'Let's get some water on him, and inside him. Come on Barry, snap to it,' he exhorted, lapsing into English.

Slowly Noor came to. 'That's it Noor, hang in there,' said Walker in Dari again. 'How many fingers?' He held two up. The boy stared dizzily through them. 'We'd better get him down the hill.'

'But… you can't Piers. I mean… we can't. What are we going to do with him when we get down there?'

'Let's just get him down. We'll worry about that when we're there. He's got no chance up here.' There was no argument.

An hour later they reached the upper valley floor. A hundred yards to their right stood the old Semenek police post, rotting without regret in its singular repose. Or so it had seemed from high up. As they drew nearer, there appeared to be life within and beside its battered structure.

Walker saw two men sitting either side of the open door, lazily absorbing the sun's warmth like reptiles, though still tightly hunched in their petous. They showed no obvious interest in the walking party despite the boy being carried between two of them. On the corner of the old stone wall stood a younger man. He had a black beard and a keen lustre in his eyes. He wore chocolate-brown shalwar kameez, with a buttonless dark grey worsted waistcoat, and had an AK-47 slung over one shoulder. This man, he saw, followed their progress as a stag watches a hiker, alert to the intrusion but as yet unwilling to challenge or run from it.

'And what the fuck do we do with him now then, eh, Piers?' said Ferguson angrily.

'We leave him. He's got some water. He has family down there if I followed his directions right. We'll plant him in the shade here, by the stream. He's looking a little stronger. What else should we have done?'

Ferguson didn't answer. He knew what he would have done.

'Listen, Barry. We haven't done anything materially wrong – yet. If we get caught now, it'll be a little uncomfortable sure, but that's all.'

They tramped on along the flat basin of the valley towards Paniger, some five miles upstream. Were it not for their efforts of the previous sleepless night and the inner tension bubbling just below the surface, the Britons might have enjoyed the beauty of this rarely seen patch of ground, where autumn rose hips rambled up decrepit stone walling and purple poppies swayed above buckthorn bushes laden with berries.

An hour later, they heard a shot behind them. Then another. And then two long bursts. *'Here we fucking go,'* thought Ferguson, with some bitterness. *'In the middle of God knows where – and now…'* Ferguson turned and walked backwards, seeing at once the lone chocolate figure of the Semenek youth following half a mile behind. He turned back,

'We've company, boys.'

'I know. The boy,' said Bashir breezily. 'He follows like a stray dog.'

'OK – so what do we do now?' asked Ferguson, striding level with Bashir. 'And the shots? Pigeons, huh?' he laughed angrily.

'We relax, Barry,' said Walker.

'In a moment we will stop – we must stop else he will be suspicious. We will pray. I will lead the prayers and you will follow – as we practised in Peshawar.'

'He'll become suspicious will he, eh? What about the boy you just dumped? A boy who heard us speaking in English?'

'Now, Barry, will you step back and remember your lines like a good mute.' Ferguson dropped back.

Paniger was nothing more than a tiny hamlet – five shepherds' huts of mud and stone set off beside the loch.

At the lochside three young girls had been laundering their clothes. On seeing the men coming towards them they hurriedly gathered up their dripping bundles and started off towards the huts with gambolling strides. Ferguson's heart beat a little faster. Suddenly he felt naked as the first two girls, with an embarrassed titter, tucked their faces into their left shoulders, quickly swinging their long dark hair across briefly glimpsed brown cheeks like a curtain.

He wondered whether they were laughing at him. He found himself staring at the girls, and saw that the last flashed a coquettish smile at Bashir as he drew level with her. Her limpid jade eyes, set perfectly in rosy brown chipmunk cheeks, sparkled in the sunlight. A teasing smile spread momentarily across her face, and then it was gone, as if in a dream. She raced on to catch the leading girl, giggling as she ran and gathering up her long black dress between her legs.

'That's a rare sight indeed, Barry,' said Walker. 'That'll probably be the last female face you'll see till you get home. They'll be wild up here and don't always behave as the mullahs would have 'em do when there's no-one about.'

At the edge of the loch they disturbed a gaggle of green sandpipers, which bobbed away from them along the shoreline. From their knapsacks the three men retrieved their petous and laid them on the dirt in front of them, Walker and Ferguson beside each other, and Bashir slightly in front, all facing the notional direction of Mecca. Then they knelt in prayer.

Out of the corner of his eye, Ferguson could see their solo Afghan watch them perform their rituals. The youth was less than one hundred yards away now. He detected a distrustful countenance about his face, or was it he who was distrustful? Perhaps they were all distrustful for all he knew. His unease made his own silent invocations to his unknown god more pious.

He and his brother had always got the giggles on the rare occasions that the family went to church; their cheeks fit to burst. Now the muscles in his cheeks were taut with fear, and drained of colour beneath the walnut-permatan. He was nervous. He felt alone and weakened by the silent part that he would have to play from here on in. With all the studious intensity of a Hamlet, he performed to his singular audience.

He began to pray, 'I know that I ain't been much of a believer, an' I'm sorry for that, but if you'd just give me an' Piers here a break so that we can…' He shot a sideways glance at the Afghan, now stationary and standing loosely beside one of the shepherds' huts. The man was staring at the three of them – just staring, with a grubby set of worry beads dangling from his right index finger.

Ferguson genuflected again with the willowy and controlled elasticity of a seasoned worshipper, and prayed that his disguise would hold up… 'An' then, I swear, I'll never get mixed up with these carpet kissing antics again in all my life – I swear it.' And then, as an afterthought, 'An' I'll even go to church when we get back.'

Over the brow of the hill to their fore, Ferguson saw a small shepherd boy swishing his flock of twenty fat-tailed sheep along the grassy edge of a stream. He was a tall boy with lanky strides, and a worn kalim satchel hanging from his shoulder by a single cord. It bumped against his left hip as he stepped out to cut off the escape-route of a determined beast. Ferguson surreptitiously looked up at the surrounding crown of peaks, and was distracted by thoughts of his youth back home in the Dales.

He remembered the first time that he had seen the after-effects of a fox's foray amongst a field of newborn lambs. The half-dozen lifeless bodies strewn any-old-how in one corner, as if sleeping peacefully save for the signature of blood on the soft, tightly-knit curls of fleece around their necks. Some had a transfixing stare of glassy-blue, others only a hollow socket where the hooded crows had gratefully gorged themselves.

How his father, uncle, brother and he, armed with shotguns, terriers and a spade, had encircled the fox's den in the hills. The frenetic yapping of the terriers dying away as they delved deeper into the den, and the heart-thudding moment when the fox had bolted from its back entrance and raced towards him, its sleek brush elegantly bobbing behind it, and its ears pushed back. He'd levelled his twelve-bore and halted its flight with both barrels.

It may not have been as pretty on the eye as the huntsman in their hunting pink much admired by Piers' sort but it had the same effect, only without the fuss.

Of course he'd always recognised the importance of uniforms and traditions: such things had made the regiment, and the regiment had made him. Ferguson had needed more, and indeed could give more. His upbringing had taught him all that he had applied successfully in the army – to look after what you've got and defend it from predators, and it will look after you. He had believed passionately in the army; he had believed earnestly in the justice of their collective actions. But when justice had been denied him and his ideals, he felt impelled to take his own action.

He returned to his duties: 'Dear God, help Piers here and me to complete the task that we've set ourselves. To take all the targets and to avenge the death of Stevie. An eye for an eye, an' all that.' He squinted at the Afghan before adding as a footnote: 'An' please God, let us live to tell the tale.' The Afghan retreated to make his own preparations to pray.

At the bottom of the path leading up to the Dogu-da Pass, Bashir stooped to uproot half a dozen wild onions, used by itinerant goatherds. He stuffed them into his knapsack. Ahead of them lay nothing more technical than a steep, rugged walk up from about two thousand eight hundred metres to four thousand five hundred metres, along a loose moraine path once used by traders taking fur from Badakhshan to Pakistan. Walker looked down into the valley at the islands of willow and acacia marooned amid the silvery stream of the Bashgal River. He was looking for the boy.

'He went on – maybe half an hour after we'd left. Headed west.' Bashir indicated with his arm. 'There's another pass over there – but too cold for him I guess.' At the top of the pass they rested again, before Bashir took them southwest and left, along the faintest trail, tracing the lip of the bowl that they stared into. Without recourse to the map in Ferguson's pack, Bashir picked the one dividing ridge of thirteen presented to him that led them into the tributary feeding the Tshocha River. It was by now late in the day.

'We'd better head down a bit before resting up and cooking our meal. It'll get pretty chilly up here in no time at all,' suggested Walker.

Suddenly there was a terrific explosion, which reverberated around the hills. It was accentuated in the steep rocky defile in which they found themselves. A crag-martin flew from its nest, cemented below the overhang of the cliff above them. It chirruped wildly, standing on its tail, and then retreated forlornly into its home. There was another bang, then another.

'What the hell was that?' cried Ferguson, more in surprise than fear. Walker shrugged his shoulders and turned to see Bashir scrambling down the tiny path.

At the end of the rockface, Bashir peered round the corner, withdrawing at once as another loud explosion echoed about their ears. He signalled for the Britons to join him.

At the head of a deep sluggish pool of water stood an Afghan man with a block of plastic explosive in his right hand, a smoking length of fuse trailing from it. The man hurled it into the water with a looping toss that sent the block and fuse spinning like a catherine wheel. Bashir didn't see the plop, but a splurge of water mushroomed from the river's surface followed by another imperious boom, which carried behind it the joyful high-pitched chattering of a line of five Afghan men thigh-deep across the tail of the pool, looking more like slip catchers than fishermen.

'My cousin Safiola, by the Grace of Allah,' twinkled their little Afghan guide, who then strode out into the open ground towards the poachers.

Chapter 9

Sher Wali rested his dented brass telescope on his fat belly. It had been seized from a peripatetic Scot long ago and then, over time, wrested from successive bands of brigands, passed on like a relay baton. Leaning against a boulder high up in the scrubby Anjoman Valley he stretched his arms forward like a rower. Relieved from watching the camel trains advance, his single good eye twitched erratically in spasms.

Sher Wali was a predator who fed off the lumbering caravans, following centuries-old traditions and routes. He had the physiognomy of both raptor and brigand: a brown leather patch covered the socket of his left eye, lost as part and parcel of his vocation; a huge beakish nose – like a tin-opener – hung over thick, black handle-bar moustaches, and an unshaven chin and cheeks. His mouth was like a post box, from which a squat fleshy pink tongue tickled his protruding bottom lip thoughtfully. He adjusted the crossed canvas-pouched bandoliers that doubled as a bra for his flabby chest, his brown eye twinkling with the inward satisfaction of a master at work – ready to pounce by expending the minimum of effort.

It was a bakingly hot day, though no hotter than usual. In the heat haze in the valley floor below, the first of three caravans headed westwards. There was barely discernible movement through an enveloping dust cloud pushed on by the faintest of breezes. Through his telescope he counted fourteen camels. He could see that beneath black carpets and jute sacks the panniers carried wooden crates. The leader, splendid in a white turban, broke from the rear of the cloud on a chestnut mare. He gesticulated broadly, trying to coax on the tail of the caravan. The stoic faces of an antediluvian breed seemed to rock gently to an unheard beat. The Anjoman River glistened in the midday sun as it writhed alongside the walking party. Occasional oxbow lakes pricked the line like musical notes.

In a pocket of ground behind Sher Wali the killer group of his ambush party chattered merrily, whilst Azip, a spindly youth, prepared their lunch of boiled rice and afghan stew. Steam curled up from the communal pot, around which a formation of flies twisted acrobatically. They were brushed aside by hands as well as the tails of twelve hardy mountain-ponies that hugged the cool of the shady rocks.

The men wore predominantly dun-coloured clothing and patchy beards and beside each lay his AK-47 and bandoliers. Mousa, the second-in-command, was a short, stocky fellow with a jolly face partially hidden by youthful wisps of beard. He broke from the group and settled next to Sher Wali.

'Are they in this caravan?' he asked.

'No. Not this one,' he replied in a deep sonorous growl.

'Maybe the one behind, then?'

'Maybe. Or maybe the one after. Who can tell in this heat.' Sher Wali tapped his rumbling stomach with his sausage-like fingers.

'How do you know who they are?'

'I don't – but call it intuition. How many blue-eyed un-Afghan looking types do you know who suddenly appear in Paniger, accompanied by two Afghans, eh?'

'Surely there are many half-casts since the time of the Shuravi.'

'Come off it, Mousa. If he has a tongue it will profit us to find it. If not then so be it – his caravan will suffice.' He winked at his designate, or was it a twitch? Mousa could never be sure.

'Just how can news from sixty miles away be so ready to find your ear? Tell me this, Sher Wali.'

'Allah is merciful, is he not, Mousa? News travels as fast along the caravan route as water flows in a river,' he replied, laughing and shaking off the flies drinking the sweat from his belly. 'They came over the Dogu-da Pass: why? Why would anyone skulk through there unless in a hurry – and if so, why? And if to avoid detection – from what, my friend, from what?' He tapped his greying temple with his telescope, and then with a peremptory air scanned the valley once more.

*

Cream coloured dust cloyed the beards and clothing of the caravan as the camels marched on listlessly with lugubrious intent marked on their faces, their jaws seemingly dislocated as they chewed on hessian muzzles.

Safiola's was only a small caravan; its seven camels were bound for the Panjsher with an illicit cargo of guns hidden amongst the quilts. Kerosene lanterns swung beneath the camel's necks, whilst pewter teapots and water carriers were strapped to its baggage like charms on a gypsy. A fluffy grey mongrel puppy sat regally on top of one bundle, surveying the twelve men who walked amongst his train.

Safiola and Walker strode out at the head, Bashir and Ferguson with the middle camels, and the remainder interspersed front to rear. AK-47's were slung by the strap, or balanced by the stock across each man's shoulders, and the rear men carried switches to tap the rump of recalcitrant beasts. Long brown faces melded with their garb, some protected from the worst of the dust by the tails of their turbans. To their left, the cooling Anjoman flowed sluggishly a milky-grey. Occasional clusters of poplars and willows shaded their march.

Ferguason heard the crack as the first shots sprayed waywardly overhead. He dived to the ground, and in the same movement brought his AK-47 up to his shoulder and wriggled back to the cover afforded by the verge of the riverside track. The Afghans stood and stared up at the hillside like bemused children as another volley was loosed at them. This time it peppered the gentle escarpment to their front.

Bashir, now recognising the danger, threw himself down beside Ferguson, with his rifle trembling in his hands.

Walker had pulled Safiola down with him as he sought cover, and as the other men wrestled with their startled animals he exhorted them in Dari:

'Let 'em go! Let 'em go! Allah will look after them. Get down behind some cover.'

Ferguson watched the hillside and spotted five positions closely grouped, given away by the muzzle flashes from badly maintained weapons. Their opponents' choice of cover was poor and they didn't move from it. He hadn't fired his weapon since acquiring it but had diligently stripped it down and cleaned the working parts each evening, as well as his magazines and ammunition. Old habits died hard.

He set his sights for five hundred metres, pulled the stock tightly into his shoulder, lining up the iron sights with the most obvious bandit to him. There was hardly a breath of wind. He fired a sighting round. The shot kicked up a spray of dirt ten feet below his target and seven o'clock to it. Quickly he adjusted his aim to compensate, and fired again. His shot found the mark of the boulder that the Afghan now desperately hugged: no one was supposed to fire back in this pathetically one-sided profession. He adjusted again and fired confidently, a burst of three rounds at his target, who now reeled from behind his rock and flailed wildly like a dervish, uttering his last staccato cry as the air was crushed from his lungs. Ferguson smiled. It felt good – 'Targets will fall when hit'. He selected another bandit, who were like ducks in a shooting gallery. Another three rounds discoloured the faded turquoise pyjama shirt, crimson seeping fast through the pastels of dust and blue.

Walker found himself similarly engaged as the bandits found their range. The powder surface of the track absorbed the bullets and kicked up a pall of smoke, making marking his targets trickier by the minute. Though the incoming fire was so far ineffective, he realised that to stay where they were would mean eventually being knocked off as they ran out of ammunition – they had only a hundred rounds per man, and to move into the open would be suicidal. He had gained a quick impression that his co-defendants were not the most competent rifle shots. They lacked fire discipline, and though none of them had been hit, they seemed to know only one way to respond, and that was to fire blindly through the smoke into the hillside.

'Stop firing!' he cried out in Dari at the top of his voice. 'Only fire at what you can see is a bandit.' Madly the firing continued. 'Will you bloody stop firing!' he screamed, and like a cowed dog they stopped as one. 'Now, only fire single shots at what you can see.' It was like dealing with delinquents. When, after a pause, the firefight continued in a more considered fashion, Walker leopard crawled beneath the verge and line of fire until he came to Safiola.

'What happens now?' he asked, breathless and sweating, the dust running down his face in rivers.

'Usually we give up,' said Safiola meekly.

'Well, not this time. Who are your best shots?'

'Habib, Hadi – maybe. No one I suppose,' he replied quietly, remaining outwardly calm, scanning the rocks above him.

'OK, well we've gotta do something. If we don't we die, and I don't think that's what Allah's got planned for us today. I'm gonna take Habib, Hadi and Bashir with me and I want you to stay here and keep their heads down.' He animated with his hands what he wanted Safiola to do.

'But where will you go?'

'We'll work our way back, and then up the gully over there.' He motioned with his head. 'Then we'll roll 'em up *Insha'Allah*.' He lifted his turban to scratch his scalp. 'You OK with that?' The camel driver nodded. 'If all goes well we'll be up there in ten minutes.'

Walker slunk back behind the prostrate men, rudely grabbing Habib and Hadi, and urging them to follow him. The Afghans looked back at Safiola for confirmation, who shooed them off as if sending his reluctant children into the madrassa. Walker eased himself between Bashir and Ferguson on the lip of the verge, both now in the thick of the firefight. In English he said,

'These two behind me and Bashir will go up that re-entrant and then roll 'em up from the flank. I want you to stay behind with the fire support. They've got no discipline and little ammo left, plus they don't seem too capable of hitting anything. But you and Safiola 'ave gotta keep their heads down. It won't take long.' He winked at Ferguson and looked behind at the two Afghans, incredulous at hearing a foreign tongue spoken – Hadi all the time smiling boyishly at Ferguson.

The mouth of the gully was shallow where it fanned out, and its bed was of small, sharp shards of slate. The four men tumbled into it and tucked themselves against the lip of the dried-out bed. Walker indicated that they were to follow him up the gully. He shuffled along on his knees and left forearm, his right arm cradling his weapon. He didn't look back.

The nullah deepened, and the detritus in its bed became more solid, angular and larger, which he moved through at a crouched run. The firefight continued to his left but gradually drifted from his ears as concentration and adrenalin took control. He had spotted a single mulberry tree on the precipice of the nullah, five hundred yards up it, and had measured it to be in line with the enemy. The nullah swung sharply to the right. He threw himself against the buttress and inched his head around to see that the way ahead was clear. He turned back to see the three Afghans frozen like statues against their cover.

'Come forward,' he whispered urgently in Dari. 'Bashir – you and Hadi head for the next corner where it turns to the left. If it's clear, signal like this.' He demonstrated the thumbs-up. 'Now, go quickly.'

Moments later the signal came and the four re-grouped. One hundred yards ahead of them, Walker spied the top of the mulberry tree. 'That's where we're going.'

He scrambled up the crumbling steep wall of the gorge, dislodging great clods of red-earth and rocks. He levered his head over the top and saw that the front was clear. His ears drew his eyes to the bandits' firing, only fifty yards down the hill. It was evident that no one person in the enemy position was taking control of the situation, and they fired more with fear than control. Bashir joined him on the edge.

'Bashir – you take Hadi to the cover of that scrub over there.' Like gun dogs the two men sprinted across the ten yards of open ground and dived into firing positions. '*You learn fast in this game,*' thought Walker with a wry smile. He tapped Habib and told him to follow in his wake to join them.

He could see the river below, and Safiola's men holding their position, and then looked across to the bandits and counted seven men squatting and lying behind rocks spread over fifty yards. He noted four bloodied corpses. Behind them, huddled beneath the rock face, he counted eleven horses shying at every shot, pawing at the ground and blowing hard through their nostrils. He calculated that there would be no one else.

The four men now lay shoulder to shoulder facing their enemy. The ground between them offered sparse cover.

'Now when I fire,' he whispered, 'I want you, Habib, to kill the nearest bandit, and you Hadi the one next to him – the one with a face like a cockerel, and you Bashir, the pretty one in pink. You got that?' The three Afghans smiled back at him with inane excitement. '*Bloody hell,*' he thought, '*I'm lumbered with flaming idiots!*' He paused. 'Then we're gonna move through these bastards in pairs. When I say 'Go' – Bashir and Hadi are to make sure that the first man is dead. Habib and I'll cover you from here. You understand? Simple shooting – save your ammunition.' Still they smiled, nodding now. 'Then Habib and I will come through you to the next one. Just don't shoot us.'

He settled his position, aligning his body to his target, the furthest Afghan, a young man with jowly features, who if any was the leader. He controlled his breathing and as he exhaled he squeezed the trigger. He looked over the barrel to see Mousa slump forward as his Chitrali cap lifted with the severance of his cranium and dropped again like a conjurer catching an egg in a paper bag. He was onto his second target as the others opened fire, killing two more, and Bashir only surprising the third with a shot that sailed harmlessly overhead.

'Go! Go! Go!' Walker pushed Bashir roughly forward.

*

The firing stopped and their enemy had been destroyed. Walker looked back at his three comrades, shaking, jabbering and astounded by what they had seen and been party to. He felt relieved and yet filled with dread such misfortune should have struck them this early in their quest. But it wasn't over. He looked down to signal to Ferguson only to see his comrade and Safiola's remaining caravan captured by a flanking movement.

*

Walker had no idea how it had happened, though it was self-evident that the incensed rabble sent to fetch them down must be connected to the men he had just accounted for. The bandits' blood was up; fear, panic and anger demonstrating themselves in shrieked ejaculations of invective and bullying commands. Rifles were pointed at them, with barrels weaving figures of eight in eager and unsteady hands. Habib and Hadi cowered as butts smacked across the backs of their necks, pushing them down the rock-strewn slope. Bashir drew strength from Walker, who solemnly did as he was told. Impassive calmness settled on his face and an inward determination steeled him to make the best of the ominous hand dealt to him.

At the bottom of the hill, Sher Wali fixed the four men with his evil eye, but was unable to detect a trace of foreignness in any of them.

'Which is the ferangi?' he commanded. None spoke up, each keeping counsel with the ground at their feet. Sher Wali pulled his horse away to the main group.

'Search the baggage thoroughly,' he ordered to the men securing the camels.

The two Britons did not look at each other. There was the faintest chance that they might get away with it if no one said anything, especially Ferguson.

But this wasn't like an SAS operation, or indeed a training exercise where the mission was the first priority. Their mission was self-serving, and now seemed a fool's errand. Did it really matter that justice, their own brand of justice, was served on Connor and Murphy? It had seemed so when the British government saw fit to release them in a horse-trading exercise with the Republicans. Now that their very lives dangled from the whim of some mad road-side despot, maddened more by the slaughter that they had activated on his men – did it matter now? Was he, Piers Walker, a principled, well-educated Scot, really any better than the man that now held his life in the balance when he himself had stooped to such base instinct? Jenny, his father, his high-minded ethics, his life even – tossed away on the rawest of human emotions – revenge. He felt as low as his captors.

Sher Wali was called to the search, and returned with Ferguson's knapsack, from which he pulled, like an eminent magician, his obviously foreign walking boots, and threw them to the ground in front of him. A sinister smile broke beneath his moustache, lifting one side of it like a death slide.

'And what would a mute,' – he spat the word with contempt and followed it with a filthy black stream of phlegm, discoloured by the naswah that he chewed '…would a mute have use for this, eh?' He hurled a satellite telephone to the ground, shattering it. 'The game is up my friend.'

Walker tried to step forward, but his way was immediately barred by one of Sher Wali's men. 'We're journalists,' he pleaded in Dari, now throwing himself at Sher Wali's horse. 'I am an Afghan from Jebel-Saraj, and this man,' he pointed at Ferguson, 'is a British journalist from the *Times* of London.' He was good, damned good, whatever he was up to, thought the now denuded Ferguson.

*

For four days and nights the party of horsemen had trekked across country, following little-used shepherd's tracks to keep out of sight. Tied to the pommels of their saddles, Bashir, Walker and Ferguson had been led, bobbing uncomfortably like flotsam on a storm-tossed sea. No friend of the Taliban, Sher Wali sought to manoeuvre his expensive prey into the pernicious and well-paying hands of General Dostum, the Uzbek warlord of the north.

On the fourth evening they had settled in the relative calm of a corrie to the north of the Khawak Pass, which looked west into the Andarab Valley and provided scratchy grazing for their horses. The Khawak Pass was a wind-parched plateau, across which Alexander had marched his army in the spring of 328 BC, and was dwarfed by the sensuous crags of the Hindu Kush. It was a pass that Walker and Bashir had crossed previously in freer times, in Alexander's footsteps. Now Walker sat slumped forward, tied around the waist to his two companions, dejected, demoralised and exhausted.

Yet with every march westwards hope flickered that they might yet escape, for at the end of the Andarab lay the entrance to Kamir's fiefdom, and the country and its people grew more familiar each day. If the opportunity arose they must take it, and if not then engineer it. But now he was tired and malnourished. The journey and the beatings from the bandits, often high on Afghan black hashish, had wearied him considerably. He looked up mournfully to survey the campsite being set up and a black mood descended upon him. Alexander had been driven to this place by personal ambitions of greatness, Walker by the folly of retribution.

The unsaddled horses had been left to graze. The cook stood watch over his crackling fire whilst two men produced bundles of sticks for him. Near the fire a barbaric council crouched around Sher Wali, AK-47s resting across their knees as they squatted, while two unforgiving-looking youths guarded the prisoners, with dilated pupils and weapons pointing lazily at them across supple hips.

Sher Wali was agitated, drawing lines in the dirt with a twig and jabbing at his map. He spat out his naswah, heaved his bulk up, and began to lead the procession towards the captives.

Walker felt the clatter of horses' hooves in the ground. He discerned a change in their own horses, which now looked up with ears pricked. Finally he heard the troop approach the encampment. He heard the heavy blowing and snorting of the posse, and then saw the first of twenty Uzbek horsemen crest the lip of the corrie. It was a surreal televisual moment as the horsemen fanned out across the pocket with their rifles raised to the perpendicular like tomahawks, looking like well-drilled Red Indians in a spaghetti western. Their leader, who rode a grey mare, trotted forward and pulled up by the fire in front of Sher Wali. He jumped to the ground with aplomb, and then gripped the one-eyed bandit by both shoulders, shook him, and kissed him on both cheeks, smiling copious rotten teeth as he did so.

'Sher Wali, you look, hmm, how shall I say, well – well, hard done by for one who lives off the fat of the land.' He patted the distended belly of the brigand, throwing his head back and laughing out loud.

'And you my friend, Halam, you don't do too bad yourself,' he replied, prodding his old acquaintance's plump tummy, which prevented his sheepskin waistcoat from meeting.

The Uzbek was an immensely powerful man; at five feet eight inches tall he was built like a prop forward, his neck the size of a tree trunk. He had a chubby, Mongoloid face with long trailing moustaches and a flimsy goatee beard. His thin eyes twinkled with mischief and his whole demeanour was one of steely merriment. He wore an astrakhan cap at a jaunty angle like a World War II pilot might have done. He had baggy white jodhpurs tucked into heavy leather riding boots like wellingtons, and a great sash of crimson cotton cloth wrapped around his waist in a cummerbund. He looked across to the prisoners.

'And who are your guests?'

'Journalists,' Sher Wali said, ejecting more naswah. 'The ferangi is from England. The two Afghans are working for him. They killed seven of my men in the Anjoman.' Halam raised an eyebrow quizzically and whistled. 'They will pay,' uttered Sher Wali, spitting out more of the dark phlegm.

'Indeed they must,' Halam muttered to himself, eyeing them more closely with villainous intent creasing his smooth features. The three men stared at the advancing Uzbek with tired eyes. This new development was not a portentous one.

The Uzbek squatted in front of them with Sher Wali standing at his back. As if at a Highland sheep sale, he mentally priced the captives, taking in their deportment, what intelligence he could glean from their eyes and brows and their strength from their jaws, arms and frames.

Ferguson met his gaze with as much resolution as he could muster. The Uzbek did not linger on him, instead he moved onto Walker, narrowing his already slanted eyes as if pained, sizing up the would-be Afghan from Jebel-Saraj. Walker stared indifferently away from him. Halam did not bother to inspect Bashir, and rising, turned to his friend and led him away to the fire with an arm around his shoulder.

'Tell me Sher Wali, what do you expect to get for these men?'

'I don't know exactly. Trading ferangis isn't my usual thing. But I was thinking maybe 100-lakh of Afghanis.'

'Hmm,' Halam sucked his teeth, 'maybe, maybe. But maybe not. Maybe you will lose them on the way.' He smiled. 'Why not let me take your problem away from you for say 10-lakh, and you can go back to robbing caravans, eh?' Sher Wali recognised that he was being swindled but acknowledged the sense in it. Hostage taking wasn't his game.

'Well, it is considerate of you to think of helping me out, but remember that they killed my men. I feel aggrieved – severely so.'

'And if you took your anger out on them what would it pay you, huh?'

'An eye for an eye—' he faltered, suddenly feeling a little self-conscious. Halam smiled kindly.

'You will gain precisely nothing, my friend. My way is your way: I'll take them off your hands and treat them with all the hospitality due them, and you – you will get a fair price for no more hassle, and no threat of loss.' He looked discreetly across to his horsemen to emphasise his point.

'You are right, you old rascal. Come – share our home for tonight and our bread, and we'll settle on a price in the morning.'

Halam looked over his shoulder at the three prisoners and smiled a hideous yellow smile.

Chapter 10

A genial gathering of men rested their satisfied bellies in front of depleted piles of pilau, goat kebabs and chicken carcasses. They sat on woollen Afghan rugs, under the awning of an open-sided marquee erected on a small plateau beneath a shimmering array of stars. The music of Bon Jovi blared from a portable stereo cassette player. Eyes were glazed, pupils dilated and a comfortably numb feeling soothed his guests as Kamir drew deeply on his joint and blew out a smoke ring. He watched it contort upwards and then disperse.

He had a stumpy frame – five foot seven inches – and carried a noticeable excess of weight everywhere, though his youth denied any impression of being unfit. His face, clean-shaven with a tidy black moustache, was round and jolly; his narrow brown eyes, even when stoned, conveyed intelligence and authority. He wore a cream pyjama suit with gold embroidered cuffs, and open brown-leather sandals, which he tucked, cross-legged, under his knees. He had a stiff, upright back as if once trained by an overbearing English nanny rather than the ladies from the hills who had reared him. Two callow, whippet-like youths, their mongoloid features cowed in his presence, stood outside the tent awaiting his godlike command. His guests lay strewn around the feast, arranged in a strict hierarchy.

Kamir sucked on his joint again and with pained pleasure passed it to Piers Walker:

'And now my friend we are even,' he said, nodding towards the comatose figure of Halam sprawled on his back against a lavishly silk tasselled cushion.

Walker nodded his head with mock servility. 'Why thank you, kind sir, but I reckon that we'd have been just fine on our own.' His eyes watered as he smoked the joint of Afghan black dope, which Kamir had often bragged was *'the best in the country'*. 'That one-eyed bandit seemed pretty glad to off-load us – and you forget we had already reduced the odds in our favour. So shall we say that the debt is only half paid, my friend?'

'Ho! You have lived with us too long! Or maybe too little, huh? Imagine if you had been sold to the Taliban? Or that turncoat Dostum? Not such a holiday for you and your friend then, eh?' Kamir screwed his eyes up, leant a little closer and smiled, 'Assuming that it is a holiday that you are here for?'

Walker ignored the implication. 'How goes it with the Taliban these days? What do they actually want from Afghanistan?'

'They want it all.' Kamir rolled his eyes heavenwards. 'They want to bring us all under their yoke. After all, the last century in my country has seen only conflict, conflict between the mullahs and the modernisers: Mohammed Daoud, Taraki, Hafizullah Amin, Babrak Karmal, and of course the Shuravi. It was always so. Since the Shuravi left in eighty-nine there has been a sort of idealist-fuelled fighting for the heart and soul of Afghanistan. But like a game of buzkashi, the goat has been ripped to pieces. It seems that the mullahs have won the day – for now.'

'But you know they'll never be able to wrest total control of the country and to rule it theocratically. They can't assert themselves on the countryside without some form of modernisation, if only in infrastructure.'

Kamir shrugged.

'To do that will mean opening up to the West, which will weaken their stance. If they know that, they won't budge, and if that happens you'll continue as you always have,' said Walker.

'Insha'Allah,' Kamir replied with subdued hope. 'But the ways of these people are primitive, ignorant, suspicious, superstitious even, and bound to the will of the mullah. Gradually it will seep through us all like a cancer.'

'Then either way you lose what you've got. With the mullahs you convert to their ways or be damned, or retreat. And modernisation will emancipate the people and you will lose your power. Your old ways will be considered anachronistic. Halam over there – his ways of plundering what he likes will not be tolerated. Your flunkies – they too will go. I have seen it in my own country. I have read it in the history books of many cultures. You cannot stand still.'

Kamir stared fixedly at the flies settling on the detritus of pilau. 'It's funny,' he mused, 'my father sent me to Great Britain when the Shuravis took control. And then as the last one crossed the Amu Darya he called me back to help him, my family and our people, to protect our and their interests from the free-for-all.' Walker handed him back the joint. 'It wasn't always this brutal. I remember the parties in Kabul, when even Heckmatyr and the rest of them joined in, before they found angst in their soul and riled against the Shuravi and now America. And now – well now we have to protect our ways against the Sharia law imposed by a bunch of Pakistani-puppet-poofters who turn their noses up against this, this and this.' He pointed to his stereo, the joint in his hand, and the bottle of Jack Daniels lying beside him. 'But if we become a secular state, well my friend you may be right, and that too will do for my people.'

Watching all the while, Ferguson had been leaning on one arm against a heap of cushions. 'You two are like two peas in a pod, you know that?' he interjected. 'Fathers, families, people, paternalism: you're so damned altruistic.' Kamir looked at him blankly, not understanding the word, and then retorted:

'But isn't it worth fighting for? What you believe in? What nurtured you and your way of life? Look around you in the morning. It's not such a bad place. There's no litter, no thieving; there's respect and deference. There's community.'

'An' what about the Taliban? Aren't they trying to do the same thing, only to the whole country?'

'And good luck to them. Just don't intrude on us, is what we say. They're setting out to destroy the great Buddhas of Bamyan, you know?'

'As cultures have done time after time before them,' said Walker, mulling over this thought. 'Again, in my country we did this with the Reformation, with Cromwell; I daresay we're doing it again now.'

'And the Afghans the same, I know,' said Kamir quietly. 'Mahmud raided India twelve times. Did you know that? In some mad frenzy he removed the idol and the gates from Kathiawar.' He sipped from a glass of iced Jack Daniels. 'The people of Kathiawar fought to save their idol and their gates...'

'As did the Indians from the Mongols, and the Mongols from Islam. Time doesn't stand still,' said Walker.

'It would be funny, if not so tragic. The Taliban started out as a bunch of do-gooders, pained by the corruption and wrong that they saw. You have a quaint folklore I remember of Robin Hood – well they're no different from him, except not so merry. But now they find themselves in charge of the country and have no idea how to run it. They're – how you say – Santa Claus?'

'Sanctimonious?' suggested Walker with a smile.

'Exactly – only in the extreme,' said Kamir without embarrassment.

'They've brought stability,' proffered Walker.

'At a price. The price of fear.'

'Medicine is often distasteful. Before them remember that you had carnage.'

'Only in the cities, towns and on the frontlines. Elsewhere life went on as before.'

'As may be. Now they are providing structure where there was none, and from that you can rebuild, remould the country into some form,' said Walker without passion.

'An' what about the terrorist training camps they allow?' opposed Ferguson.

'They keep it pretty secret – as indeed anyone would; it's like a family embarrassment. Osama bin Laden and Mullah Omah have some weird thing going on. Bin Laden's helped the Taliban financially, ideologically and militarily, but there are signs that cracks are beginning to appear in the relationship. You see, the Arabs look down on the Afghans, thinking them unclean and backward. The Taliban begin to realise that not only are they being used – I mean bin Laden has free rein to do whatever dark deeds he wants to – but, I also reckon that the mullahs are beginning to realise that they need the West more than the terrorists. One of them must give; they are not mutually binding sympathies. We shall see; bin Laden is a crafty devil by all accounts.'

'You've not met him?'

'No – but I know those who have.'

'An' what's he 'ere for?'

'Some sort of holy war. He's a holy fool if you ask me, and yet, though he has none of the authority of the mullahs, he seems to have their ear – at least the more fundamentalist ones. He reckons that he's defeated one superpower, the Shuravi, when fighting here in the eighties – that is if he actually did any fighting. And the 'Great Satan', America, is next. His rhetoric about Saudi Arabia, Palestine and Iraq is all bullshit. Just clever PR to incite more people to his cause. He's up himself; power-crazy if you ask me.' Kamir twirled his right forefinger around his temple.

Walker leant closer to Kamir's ear: 'Do you know where and how they operate? I mean, do you get to hear what's going on on the other side?'

'Of course. I have people who know people, if you know what I mean,' he chuckled. 'And so do they, though currently I am way down their list of interesting people. Massoud takes up most of their energies.'

'We didn't exactly walk a couple of hundred miles just to catch up with you, my old friend,' said Walker, as Kamir feigned surprise. 'You see, Barry and I are looking for a couple of people. Irish people. We know that they entered the country in the last couple of weeks, and we know that they'll be here for a couple of months – staying with friends as it were. Would you be able to help us find them?'

'These Irish people, they are friends of yours?'

'Old acquaintances shall we say.' Walker smiled diffidently. 'They killed a friend of ours.'

Kamir erupted in laughter, throwing his head back and then toppling onto his cushions whilst clutching his tummy. 'Oh, Piers! Truly you have been amongst us too long, my friend.'

*

Walker woke on a balcony overlooking a once sumptuous courtyard, where the vegetation now distorted the ancient frieze, like ice in a granite fissure. Two mastiffs prowled towards each other at the far end of the courtyard like sentries outside Buckingham Palace. An Ishmaeli guard was dozing in a bamboo chair beside a pair of iron trellis gates. It was a cool, cloudless morning.

He saw the three MiGs cut low through the valley towards them like bluebottles. He heard, and then felt, the boom of noise as they passed over his head. Then he felt the wave of the three wayward five hundred kilogram bombs that they dropped. A tardy and laconic *pop-pop-pop-pop* followed as the Shilka 23mm anti-aircraft guns aimlessly pursued the MiGs. He saw a solitary plume of smoke rise above the courtyard wall like a cypress tree. It was all too familiar.

'What the fuck was that?' Ferguson had leapt from his sleeping bag, grabbed his AK-47 and was now adopting a fire-position in the recess of the room.

'Relax. Just a wake up call,' laughed Walker, picking up his towel from a wicker stool. 'They won't be back. Probably returning from a raid against Massoud and needed to offload their bombs to look good.'

Ferguson rubbed the sleep from his eyes and leant on the balcony railings. He waved at Kamir as he came through the gates where the guard – probably the sole beneficiary of the MiGs' sortie – now stood, fully awake and prepared for his duties.

'The bastards have hit my swimming pool again. That's why I don't fill it up,' bemoaned Kamir as he joined the Britons and Bashir on the balcony.

'Thought you said that you weren't on the Taliban's invite list?' quizzed Ferguson sardonically.

'I'm not – but it's nice to be remembered once in a while,' he chortled, looking across to the smoke rising from his pool. He turned to Ferguson and smiled ruefully, 'Or maybe it's you that has attracted their attention.'

'No one knows we're here.'

'No one except my people, Halam's people, Sher Wali – and he's pretty pissed with you – and whoever drew you to Sher Wali's beady eye.' He paused. 'How do you think Halam found you?'

'But they don't know who we are, or why we're here.'

'And I don't know who your friends are, or who their friends are – not that I want to know too much about them. You see what I mean?' Ferguson looked at Walker who shrugged his shoulders. 'Anyway, I have set the wheels in motion to see if we can locate your friends for you; it shouldn't prove too difficult. In the meantime, let's get some breakfast, and then Piers I'd be glad to show off my opium rehabilitation clinic.'

'What is this? Some kind of philanthropic Olympiad or what?' expostulated Ferguson.

'You forget, my friend, that in this small fiefdom my people look to my father and I to provide for them. In your country it is the same is it not? Your Queen Elizabeth provides for her people through her ministers does she not? It is simply a matter of scale.'

*

As the Land Cruiser turned into the long approach road to the Wazir Akbar Khan Hospital in Kabul, the mid-afternoon temperature had steadied at 41°C. The Taliban militia guard, seated at a trestle table festooned with AK-47's and an RPK on its bi-pod, ushered them through. The road was dusty and marked with shell holes. The grass on either side was parched yellow and littered with an array of blown gun-emplacements. The carcasses of a BMP command vehicle, its antenna rusted and limp, and a T-64 – or so Sean Connor presumed – with its turret severed from the body had been pushed onto the verge.

They pulled up under the portico, behind an ambulance disgorging its fetid assortment of humanity, some dead, some not far off. One had been maimed below the knee by a blast of some kind that had left a bleeding tissue of stump and a tourniquet around the thigh to stem the flow. Dosed with morphine the owner of this visual abhorrence stared serenely at the two Afghan porters picking him from the bottom shelf on his wood-poled canvas stretcher. It looked like an early morning scene from Smithfield Market. Connor exhaled deeply.

His taciturn escort led him into the cool foyer, with its floor a checkerboard of white and black tiles. Solicitous groups of families and friends lingered underneath and at the foot of the rose-coloured marbled stairs, where worry beads dangled and clicked from the landing balustrades. Men lay quietly on stretchers in an arcane queuing system that none grumbled about, though there were occasional cries of 'Allah!' which subsided into pained moans. Ahead of him was the first aid point – or was it the operating theatre, it wasn't immediately clear to Connor. He lingered and then moved towards it, drawing his escort with him, a morbid fascination taking over his senses. Twenty-odd beds lined the walls. In contrast to the foyer there seemed to be life rather than fear and anxiety; a buzz of activity pervaded, and a murmur of noise: patients groaning, doctors trying to assert command over chaos and life itself. The struggle that he witnessed with rictus-like incredulity was epitomised in the bed nearest him.

A lank, bearded doctor in washed blue coveralls soaked in sweat and caked in blood, stood at the end of the patient's bed smoking a cigarette. A nurse cut through the bloody clothing of a young Afghan whose left side had been peppered with shrapnel from a land mine. The doctor wore no gloves as he inspected the wounds with some form of probe, the ash from his cigarette defying gravity as it arced over the largest gash. He muttered something to the nurse before moving onto the next bed. The nurse summoned a trolley and had the man rudely placed on it, leaving his blood to congeal on the mattress – a posse of flies hung over it before swooping. Another nurse slopped a bucket of detergent-water over the mattress and swabbed it down with a grotty looking cloth. The waste ran off into an open drain pursued by the flies, which settled on the gungy grill to drink in the ambrosia. Another patient was claimed from the foyer as the young man was wheeled off. Connor felt a tug at his sleeve and his escort motioned with his head that it was time to move on.

In the basement, the light and air had been sanitised but both were artificial, and a strong smell of iodine overpowered his senses. The escort pointed to the entrance and then held back to allow him to enter alone. He pushed through the stiff, scratched, opaque plastic sheeting – as if entering an abattoir. In the middle of this otherwise empty ward of four beds lay Declan Murphy, napping in surprisingly clean white cotton sheets, and with a drip attached to his left arm. He perked up immediately on seeing Connor, raising himself on his elbows and then pulling up the sheet to cover his torso.

'Tank God for de NHS, is all I can say, Seany. You ain't never seen anyting like it in all your time.'

'Kabul brings out dose latent Brit sympathies in de Murphy blood,' teased Connor as he seated himself at the end of the bed. He tapped his stomach, adding, 'An' how's yoursel? – Still wallowing in ya sel' inflicted intestinal wounds, are ya?'

'I dunno what ya're crowin' about. It'll soon enuff be yoursel lyin' here. D'ya know dis place used to be a target for de gunners years ago when de Muj were rippin' Kabul ta pieces? Pity dey didn't blow de whole focken place up if ya ask me.'

'Well ya shouldn't ha' got sick, Dec.'

'We shouldn't be here, Seany. I dunno what de man tinks he's focken playing at with dese daft buggers. Dey're focken animals, I tell ya. De food an' conditions are inhumane. I dunno what ya're laughin' at. I'll be laughin' mesel' when it's your turn, Seany, so I will. I've lost pints o' fluid – from both focken ends!' He paused before adding with theatrical indignation: 'Dey stuffed a drip into me focken arse!'

'Dat all?' said Connor, furrowing his brow comically.

'Dere was a man in de next bed yesterday. He'd had his hand chopped off for tieving. Can ya focken believe it? An' do ya know why dey do it?' Connor shook his head trying not to laugh. 'Coz dey wipe dere arses with dere left hands, an' eat with dere right.'

'So?'

'So – dey eat with dere right hand don't tey, dippin' it into the communal trough. An' if dey have only one hand dey must do everytin' with it, ya follow. So not only 'as the bugger got one focken hand – a lesson an' a mark to de world dat he'd a tief – but de poor bastard's excluded from feeding times an' his community.' He looked dolefully at Connor who had lost his grin.

'An' what does dat make us den, Dec – de beatings, tarrings, kneecappings, eh?'

The plastic door was pushed aside and Abdul Qadir, looking immaculate in white – like a starched matron – intruded on their conspiratorial conference.

'And how is the patient?' he said, squeezing a smile.

'Just fine Abdul, tanks,' lied Murphy. 'On de mend, ya know. I was just tellin' Sean here dat I was chomping at de bit to get going.

I'll be putting dis little mishap down to experience an' I'm sure dat me stomach'll be stronger for it.' He spoke with a confidence that masked the inward nervousness of a schoolboy unsure whether he had been overheard.

'Good my friends. There is no hurry, but preparations are being made for our stay in Navor. We'll head there in five days time. Doctor Kabir tells me that you should be fit for this next stage.' He smiled deprecatingly at Murphy. 'I'll give you a lift back if you like, Sean.' He turned back at the door. 'I am sorry about all of this; most unfortunate.'

'Can't be helped,' grimaced Murphy.

*

Kamir had set up an improvised shooting range in a re-entrant off the main Kayan valley. There were no flags, no wardens, no telephones with which to control proceedings; just Kamir, megaphone in one hand and bottle of beer in the other, shouting instructions at the receiving end of the range where two of his men had been timidly positioned to score the shooting and right the falling-plate targets. The firing point was not pre-determined. In the back of Kamir's white pick-up sat his coterie, the pre-chosen weaponry resting between their legs and cases of ammunitions scattered about their feet. There was an RPF7, G3s, Colt M-16s, a Dragunov sniper rifle, a Degbyarev 30 machine gun, and a Barrett M82A1 sniper rifle amongst them. The latter weapon caught Walker's eye.

'Do you see the 'Light Fifty' there, Barry?' pointing to the Barrett. 'Wouldn't that be a master stroke of irony if we could pop 'em off with that beauty.'

'What do you mean?' asked Kamir.

'In the Nineties in South Armagh, the IRA had an extremely effective sniper team that used one of these,' said Walker, relieving the Ishmaeli of the rifle. 'Rarely missed. Just one shot and then slipped away. The Yanks got a confirmed kill in the Gulf in ninety one at one thousand eight hundred metres. Our man usually knocked them off within a kilometre. It's bloody difficult to spot the firing point with one shot from that kind of distance.' He ran his fingers along the 737mm barrel, more than half the weapon's length. 'An ugly brute of a thing though isn't it? Heavy too – twelve point nine kilograms if memory serves me right.' He looked through the times ten telescopic sights. 'Fantastic. Can I have a go with this one?' he asked Kamir excitedly.

'By all means.'

'We've got two options once we know where they are – long range or close up. If long range then you don't get much better than this, though it's cumbersome to insert with. We'll see.' He settled himself on a scrubby knoll beside the pick-up and placed five rounds in the ten-round magazine. 'Barry, do us a favour and check the clock on Kamir's milometer, will you please.'

Ferguson leant into the cab, his eyes immediately picking out the satellite phone between the seats. He checked the milometer.

'One point two kilometres, Piers,' he shouted back.

Walker adjusted his sights, aligned himself to the full-body paper target, steadied his breathing, picked up the target in his scope, and squeezed the trigger as he exhaled. He had the weapon tightly gripped into his shoulder, and with the bipod firmly set, absorbed the recoil without disturbing his position. He raised his eye above the scope to see a puff of dust ten o'clock of the target, where the bullet, travelling at just less than 850-metres per second, obliterated the rock that it hit. He adjusted his sights and fired again. His third shot found its mark. The fourth knocked over the upper-body-falling-metal-plate target. His fifth sent the head plate cartwheeling into the air. Kamir applauded, his men nodding appreciatively at his skill.

The firing party turned to see a red pick-up coming towards them, leaving a trail of billowing dust in its wake. Kamir walked across to the cab, leant inside and after a brief discussion returned to Walker.

'We've found your friends, Piers. Seems that one of them has a weak constitution. I think that you might call it dysentery back home. You'll no doubt be happy to hear that he has survived the further hazards of the Wazir Akbar Hospital and that he's on the mend. My spies tell me that they are to head for Navor this week, where they are to spend some weeks watching proceedings. They claim to be journalists come to report on life under Sharia law,' he said with some amusement evident in his voice. 'So many journalists, eh!'

'When you say they – how many?' asked Ferguson.

'Two of them. Plus the Taliban and Arabs. Apparently they have been treated like royalty by their hosts.'

'If that results in dysentery I'd hate to be a peasant.'

Chapter 11

'We'll need to get down there pronto to take a squint,' said Walker, studying the map with Bashir, Ferguson and Kamir beside him, both the Brits and Kamir cradling a bottle of beer each.

'We can set up a base at Mushi,' suggested Kamir, pointing to the small town to the north of Navor. 'We should be safe enough there – not a Taliban stronghold, and from here we could pick up a ride into Navor with a melon truck or whatever's passing. My wife's cousin has an excellent little chai-khana we could stay in.' He looked round the table for approval. Ferguson was about to contend that it was a long way back to Mushi, but seeing this Kamir puffed himself up, adding, 'Of course it's forty miles from Navor, but getting back would be no problem. We could arrange to meet half way under cover of darkness, say, if you're worried about setting a pattern.'

Ferguson nodded, 'It's a start.'

Kamir was noticeably pleased with himself. 'Probably best, my friend, if you leave this bit to Piers, Bashir or better still to my people. No disrespect, but you don't exactly look like an Afghan close-up.' Ferguson smiled, knowing the Ishmaeli to be right. 'Besides, there'll be plenty to do with me. We'll need time to think of escape routes and diversions.'

Kamir's bar was retro-seventies with a distasteful predilection for Artex. The four-foot high bar curved out into the high-ceilinged room like a stage. An arch of mirrored tiles were stuck to the wall behind it, where five bottles each of Jack Daniels and Stolichnaya hung like stalactites in dispensers. Cardboard cases of bottled beer were stacked neatly beneath the bar, over which a haze of barflies hung. The omnipresent cassette-stereo stood on it, with a saturnine-looking servant positioned nearby, poised to break the peace. Around the spartan extremities of the room, Kamir's entourage – old and young – sat silently, waiting to morph into his shadow when he moved.

'What happens in Navor?' asked Ferguson.

'Not a lot. It's a quiet market town. Less than ten thousand people I guess. It's the first stop westwards from this bit of the Helmand Valley. It's fertile land – or certainly used to be before the Shuravi.'

'An' you reckon the al-Qa'eda training camp is to the south-east in this nest of hills?'

'So I believe. I have never been there myself.'

'The insertion and extraction will be pretty tricky,' Ferguson said, directing this last at Walker.

'These Arabs have night vision kit, but they're a bunch of – how you say – "Muppets"?' said Kamir, grappling with his memory for the military slang he had once picked up under Walker's influence. 'Remember, they think they're secure here. Massoud's miles away, hemmed in to the north and east. That said, I don't believe that this is a permanent camp, as they favour the east and the Pakistan border.'

'Maybe they're treating Paddy specially,' said Ferguson.

'More likely they don't want to show them what they're really up to. And we Muslims are a precious lot about our religion,' he said. He winked mischievously at Ferguson and took a swig from his beer.

'Don't underestimate their faith. A couple of infidels won't exactly mix it with these zealots and bigots and they'll want to keep the Irishmen out of sight of all but those that need to know about them, lest they be accused of hypocrisy,' rejoined Bashir.

A man of slight frame, about five-foot six inches in height, with a neatly trimmed, greying beard and clear brown eyes, shuffled diffidently to the table, twisting his Chitrali Cap with his hands as if ringing out the rain. Kamir acknowledged him by extending his right arm towards him and saying warmly in Dari:

'Boba, old man, come closer,' and in English to the others, 'Khalil was my father's bodyguard once upon a time. As brave as a lion, stubborn as a camel. Looks can be deceiving,' he added, tapping the side of his nose knowingly.

'I heard, Sahab, that your friends are interested in Navor,' he said quietly in Dari. 'It is no secret from us that your friends have 'business' with the Arabs. I know this ground like it was my garden. My father dug out and rebuilt many of the karez in the plain. As a boy I used to play in them. I would consider it an honour if I might be able to help your friends against our enemies.' He stepped back, bowed his head and waited.

'Sounds very interesting,' said Walker in English. 'These karez, are their routes known? And how safe are they?'

'What's a karez when it's at home?' asked Ferguson.

'An underground irrigation channel. Built perhaps thirteen hundred years ago by the Persians or the Afghans. The most effective way to carry water across desert regions from the mountains. They can run for some twenty-five miles. They were maintained over the years – had to be of course…'

'But then the Shuravi came and we have lost much ground; Afghanistan is no longer the breadbasket that it was once. Who knows what state these karez are in, but it's worth a look, I grant you,' cut in Kamir.

'Well if this guy knows about them, don't the Taliban or the al-Qa'eda people?' Ferguson questioned.

'Possibly, but I think on balance not. It is not their heartland.'

'An' yer man here, is he up to such a caper? Is he fit enough?'

Kamir laughed and spoke in Dari to Khalil: 'He wants to know if you are fit?' The old man smiled faintly. 'Of course he is my friend,' he continued in English, 'and what is more I would trust him with my own life.'

'OK,' said Walker with determination, 'that's settled then. Khalil and I will recce the routes and locate the camp, and you will set up a base at Mushi. We'll need some night vision kit and a scope. Would a radio be picked up by the Taliban?'

'I doubt that you'll come across much overt evidence of the Taliban, though they will have their spies everywhere. However, I doubt a radio will work. Best to stick to a couple of time plans. We'll soon know if things go wrong. But, hey, apparently no one knows that you are here, so what are you worried about!' he laughed.

'When do we start for Mushi then?' asked Ferguson.

'Patience. Safeed, more beers, and put that damned music on.' He shouted this last in Dari to the solemn-looking attendant behind the bar.

*

Beneath the drab-green army canvas, flies circled the bare torsos of the two men lying on camp beds. With arms heavy with sleep, they tried to waft them away as they dived teasingly onto their mouths and eyelids. Connor and Murphy had been dropped into the mountainous training camp by helicopter late the previous night – along with Qadir – and deposited by torchlight into their tented accommodation. Now it was half an hour prior to dawn, and the air inside, though stagnant, was tolerably cool. The tent flap was pushed back by a thirteen-year-old Afghan boy with a smooth complexion, and wide eyes that sparkled in the half-light. His bright smile became evident as he popped his head inside.

'As salaatul khairune minanaum,' he twittered merrily.

'Ah, fock off!' Murphy retorted gruffly. The boy withdrew hurriedly. 'What de bloody hell did he say?'

'He said, "Prayer is better dan sleep",' replied Connor, contemplating the poetry in the phrase.

'An' how de bloody hell do you know dat?'

'While you was having your arse probed in Kabul, I took de trouble to find out a little of what goes on. It's some sort of morning ritual dey have.'

'Well, I'd say dat dat little boy was after you for his own morning ritual. He seems to hang about us like one of dese infernal flies. He was here when we arrived. Did he ever leave?'

'Relax, Dec, or you'll not survive de next few weeks. He's been assigned to look after us by Qadir – a sort of servant if you like.' A doleful wail echoed around the training camp from a loudspeaker. 'Ah, the 'Azan', the call to prayer,' said Connor with wry satisfaction.

'You're not gonna go bush on me are ya, Seany?'

'No – but when in Rome, you might as well see it an' understand it a wee bit. Dese guys are fanatical. Dey pray five times a day, 'n if dey don't dey lock 'em up in a cave on de other side of the hills dere. Makes Father Frank back home seem like a heathen.'

'But I didn't tink dere was a mosque out here.'

'Dey don't need a mosque, Dec, just de direction o' Mecca. Besides, it's a temporary camp.'

'Aye, I noticed the lack of a shite-house yesterday evening when we got here. No wonder I've already had focken dysentery. Tere's no bloody hope for me here.' Murphy sat up in bed and rubbed his itchy scalp. He pulled on a grubby pair of khaki shorts, grabbed his towel, fumbled for his flip-flops and walked outside to find the first rosy fingers of dawn claiming the sky.

The camp, which consisted of twenty tents in two facing rows, was abuzz with people scurrying backwards and forwards from their ablutions before the Salaat Fajr – morning prayer – was performed on prayer mats in the open. He stood and stared at the scene disdainfully, farted loudly, picked up the plastic watering can that the boy had filled and left outside their tent, and headed for the designated wash-area behind their accommodation. Two tardy Muslims were still performing their wudhuu – their ritual ablutions before prayer. They were stripped down to the waist and washing their arms, hands and feet from similar watering cans to his; they rinsed their mouths, and wiped their hands and heads and trotted back to their tents. A more elderly man was squatting ten yards away, rocking gently as if in a trance, the front of his pyjama top hanging over his knees so that he looked like a weevil wearing a white skull cap. The old man looked away with embarrassment and then stood up, and the stench of fresh human excrement pierced the dawn.

'Oh my focken God. Dey're a bunch of animals,' Murphy muttered under his breath.

The sun was peeping over the rugged horizon as he returned to his tent, and the sky was turning an unimpeachable light blue. He had estimated that there were forty people in the camp, and these now gathered in groups of threes and fours to recite verses from the Qur'an. Connor still lay naked on his bed as he went inside.

'Sorry to disappoint you, 'tis only me,' said Murphy impishly, and then added gruffly, 'Does your boy bring us breakfast in bed?'

'Ah, give over will ya, Dec, you ain't humorous at dis time of de morn – if a'tall.' He rubbed his face. 'Breakfast is served outside dat mud-hut out dere – de only permanent fixture it seems of de camp. I popped in dere last night. Pretty basic.'

'You do surprise me. Some sort of earthen oven with an open fire pit, I'll bet.'

'In one.'

'An' de breakfast'll be de same shite dat gave me de shites in Kabul last week, huh?'

'You're a regular tourist guide.'

'Some sort of vile green porridge just to make de Irish feel at home. Lentils with spices – dhal dey call it, don't dey? Focken dull more like. An' de obligatory flat stale bread – well 'm sticking with de bread from now on an' claiming me rations back frae de Man when – an' it seems a big focken when right now – when we get outta dis shitehole.' He hurled his towel on to his bed as he ranted.

The tent flap was again pushed back and the sleek features of Qadir intruded. Connor hastily pulled the sheet up to his chin.

'Sorry to burst in like that,' said Qadir looking scornfully at Murphy.

'Not a'tall, Abdul. Top o' de morn to ya,' he replied with transformed geniality. 'Seany an' I were just wondering how we might fill our day in dis beautiful place, weren't we Seany?'

'Indeed,' mused Qadir. 'Well I have come to – er – fill you in as it were.' Connor sat up. 'I'll introduce you to Mustaffa in a moment. He speaks excellent English and I've asked him to be your interpreter and mentor while you are with us here. He's an old hand; he knows the camp routine, the instructors and many of those attending. You will be training the trainers, passing on your bomb-making skills and tactics. And who knows, you may learn a thing or two from us. You got all you needed in Kabul I take it?'

'Aye, we have that,' said Murphy slowly.

Qadir narrowed his eyes. 'Well there's physical training after breakfast. A run up into the hills if you fancy it.' Murphy patted his stomach and waved away the invitation.

'I tink dat Seany an' I'll give it a miss for today if you don't mind.'

'Your choice. Then there's weapons training. We've quite a little collection. Perhaps you'll find that more to your liking?'

'Indeed we might.'

'The arrangements are fairly loose. Firing takes place behind the hill beyond the cookhouse. But it's up to you – you have the early morning to make your preparations. The two hours before lunch each day are for your training of us – the programme we discussed in Kabul? Basics building up to practical exercises and assessments.'

'Dat's no problem, Abdul.'

He turned to leave, and then back again. 'And of course there's Salaat, five times a day. I am sure that you will respect our ways. Indeed you are welcome to join us if you so wish. You wouldn't be the first to convert at our camps; a year ago two former Russian Spetsnatz converted.'

'Tanks, Abdul – we'll bear dat in mind.' Connor smiled depreciatingly at him.

'Oh, and it would be as well to remember that we're not too keen on seeing too much flesh about the camp. Shorts aren't a good idea. When in Rome and all that. Now, let me introduce you to Mustaffa.' He left the tent.

'I wish I was in bloody Rome,' grumbled Murphy under his breath.

Seconds later, the tent flap was forced back. 'Gentleman, this is Mustaffa: Mustaffa, Mr Connor and Mr Murphy,' said Qadir, smiling at the Irishmen and enjoying the moment as they looked at the hard cruel face of their mentor. He was a powerful-looking man: barrel-chested, a huge neck with pulsing veins, and hands clasped behind his back like meat cleavers. His nose had been broken several times in his youth in the back streets of Cairo.

Mustaffa didn't smile and only moved his eyes as Qadir introduced him to each man. But it was his eyes – black, beady and soulless – that immediately sent an icy chill through the forced bonhomie of Murphy. Mustaffa didn't care for infidels; he made that clear without uttering a word. This was a duty that he would suffer for the greater good.

'Pleased to meet ya,' said Murphy, with false cockiness as he offered Mustaffa his hand.

The Egyptian steadfastly refused to shake it. Murphy withdrew his, wiping it on his shorts.

'Well I'll let the three of you get acquainted,' said Qadir without irony and left the tent again.

'Er... I'll be getting dressed if it's all de same to ya,' said Connor, raising his eyebrows at Mustaffa. 'We'll catch up over breakfast shall we?'

'As you wish,' replied the Egyptian in a deep, quiet voice, and departed.

'Talkative chap, dat Mustaffa, eh, Seany? Hardly de sort o' mentor dat you'd have hoped for on a trip abroad,' said Murphy quietly.

'Aye, an' he didn't look too chuffed to be looking after de likes of us,' replied Connor, searching for his shirt at the end of his bed.

'I don't suppose dat we'll be taken to de camp's fleshpots by yer man, eh, - harems don't dey call 'em in dis neck o' de woods?' said Murphy, looking ruefully at the tent flaps as they settled into place.

'Well, I've news for you dere, Dec,' said Connor sarcastically. 'Dis ain't no focken 18-30 holiday. Dey don't do women in Afghanistan dese days – well, not dat you'd notice at any rate.'

*

Piers Walker sat crossed-legged, dressed in the local garb, every inch of him acclimatised to the languid, poetic, peaceable, and brutal nature of Afghanistan. His face was tanned and leathery. The creases around his almond-shaped eyes, hooded and half-closed from the constant glare of the sun, had been etched into his skin like a relief map. He had aged beyond his years from the strain of rough living and malnourishment. His hands were walnut-brown, long and sinewy, with broken fingernails picked clean by twigs, and between his fingers there was chalky whiteness from chafing.

There's an old saying that a *'Pathan waits a thousand years for revenge'*; Walker was that Pathan. There was a deep well-spring of excitement and anticipation within him that his stoical face did not belie. He was on the cusp of settling his personal vendetta. And for Walker, being that Pathan meant that the rights and wrongs imposed by his own society had vanished as fast as the plate of kebabs in front of Kamir.

He was seated in the square attic room of the chai khana, whose only chattels were a dusty orange kalim carpet and the company of Bashir, Ferguson, Khalil, Kamir, and four of his coterie. In front of each man was a plate of goat kebabs on skewers. A tilly-lamp lit the four corners, around which moths and insects clattered. Wicker blinds were drawn across the window, shutting out the starry, moonless night that lulled the soporific town of Mushi to sleep in its steep sided cradle of hills.

Walker had drawn two sketch maps from their reconnaissance and manufactured a model of the training camp out of the oddities of the chai khana: threads from the kalim represented water-flows, cubes of kebab the tents. He used his own skewer as a pointer to demonstrate all that they had seen over the previous three days.

'I must get some more kebab before we start,' said Kamir.

'But you've had about twenty so far,' jibed Ferguson.

'Yes – but my record is twenty-nine and Aziz, my wife's cousin, will think me weak – or worse, rude – if I don't match this number.' One of his men slipped from the room, returning shortly with Aziz, timid but smiling graciously at the compliment Kamir was paying him.

'Now, shall we start?' said Walker, challenging Kamir to pay attention. He spoke in English for Ferguson's sake and for security, while Khalil stared blankly at the mysterious construction before him. The little man had been only too happy to help his master's son; anything to stop the creeping tide of the Taliban's oppressive ways. He hadn't dreamed of asking Walker why he particularly wanted to get to a position that would be able to look into the al-Qa'eda training camp. In getting him there, like an artful stalker he had gained all the gratification that he had wanted. They'd talked along the way about the old days, his father, about the karez, about the countryside, but always Walker had initiated the conversation. The old man loved his master – almost worshipped him like a god. Kamir was different of course, with his modern outlook and toys. But he was of the same lineage as Fazir Khan, and that counted for everything, and if he, an old man of countless years could help, it was his happy duty to do so.

Walker began to describe their recce.

'If the ground is so open to get to this nullah and from the col you can see into the camp, why aren't the Arabs at least watching it?' questioned Ferguson.

'Three reasons,' proposed Kamir. 'One, because they are terrorists and not conventional tacticians, two, they feel totally secure, and three – and I hate to say this – three is because they're Asiatics and too stupid and lazy.'

'My take is that Kamir's right. I wasn't surprised by what we didn't see.'

'Do you think that you could get into the camp?' asked Kamir, wiping his mouth contentedly having completed his quest.

'Of course. The cover's good, but – and it's a big but – the camp discipline is irregular: dangerously loose. I'll come to that. It's a basic camp – twenty tents; ten facing ten in a neat row east-west. There's one adobe serai with a fire here – probably the cookhouse. A wash and crap area here. But apart from the domestics it is one hundred percent some sort of training camp. We saw skill at arms sessions here, and there's a firing range around this buttress from what we heard. One small group went on a forced march in the hills with their weapons, but to the west. Then who should appear from this tent here, but Sean Connor himself – or a damned good likeness of him from that distance.'

'How far?'

'One click maybe – but with the scope we had, I'm ninety percent certain it's him.'

'So if you know one of them's there, I still don't see why you don't creep in and slit his throat?' pressed Kamir.

'Because I've no idea what goes on there at night. They're a bunch of fanatics with a great deal of firepower, but let's not discount it just yet. The only kind of order I saw were two close sentries posted here and here.' He looked around at the three English speakers. 'Any more questions on the ground and sketches?'

'How do they get their provisions into the camp? Over the hills by man-pack?'

'Good point. No, there's a vehicle track that comes in from the west up the valley. It's the only way in, and Khalil gathered that it's well guarded. The locals believe that the hills are mined.'

'A spook story,' said Kamir. 'An old mujahideen trick.'

'So what do you reckon, Baz?'

'Well, so far so good, but how the hell do we get from the karez and back to where? I mean, they ain't gonna be too chuffed if their 'A' list celebrities are hit, are they?'

'This is where you begin to wonder why we're here,' joked Walker.

'I've been wondering that since touch-down,' replied Ferguson.

'Well, I've been thinking about that too,' said Kamir with a beaming smile. 'The kuchi...'

'The what?' said Ferguson.

'Like nomads, Baz. They have ancient migratory routes that cross this part of the world irrespective of frontiers – as if they were birds.' Ferguson nodded as Walker turned his attention back to Kamir.

'The kuchi group that come this way each year are heading up from the Helmand Province right now, and by good fortune are at Markhana this very day. They come through Kayan via Mushi and Bamian every year at this time. Our people go back a long way. Sher Agha is their leader; he is like my brother.'

'Didn't know you had a brother,' said Ferguson, slowly. Kamir returned a cross look at him.

'What are you saying, Kamir?' said Walker, astonished by the Ishmaeli's impudence and put out that he would presume to involve others without consulting them.

'Well... that I have sent word that you might need their help,' he jabbered, looking round and vainly trying to elicit support in the

Briton's eyes. It wasn't reciprocated. He pressed on, now giggling nervously, 'You'll know Sher Agha if you see him – short, fat, a henna beard, bushy black eyebrows. He always wears a pink cummerbund and rides a white mountain pony...'

'What did you tell him?'

'Just that I had a couple of friends that he should look out for should they come to him.' His voice tailed off.

Chapter 12

At midnight Kamir dropped the four men at the bridge under a cloudless night sky. He negotiated a three-point turn in his pick-up truck, and then, leaning out of the window he said in a hushed voice to Walker:

'When you get back... then we are even. Khoda hafiz, may God protect you.'

The truck bit into the loose surface of the road and pulled away up the hill to Mushi. Walker watched Kamir's attendant coterie perched on the lip of its bucket, their RPGs silhouetted against a backwash of ambient red light from the brake lights, making them look like a sheath of arrows. He turned away and headed in the opposite direction, followed by Ferguson, Bashir and Khalil.

He had mentally marked a route to the opening of the karez to be navigated at night – a turn in the river, a large boulder and finally lining up a solitary weeping willow on the far bank with a dried ox-bow lake. It was a chilly night. They had wrapped themselves tightly in dun-coloured petous on the ride down to the bridge, but now they let them flap open to allow the air to circulate.

Each man carried his AK-47 slung over his shoulder. Walker also carried the Barrett in a sheepskin case strapped across his back; the telescopic sight he had carefully packaged in a polythene bag and hung from his neck in a sheepskin parcel like an amulet. Ferguson carried a scope for the Barrett in his canvas knapsack, zeroed for himself, and a mortar-fire-controller's laser, which had been tested and stowed away in a waterproof protection. Both men carried night vision sights in their spare hand.

Bashir had less far to travel and longer to wait, but being used to the elements he travelled lighter. Within his soul he bore a heavy burden for his friends, though even now he failed to totally grasp that they could with pre-meditation steal the life from a fellow man, even one who had wronged them. He had never supposed that they – civilised Westerners as he thought them – could be like an Afghan; even the Russians had retreated and not returned.

The opening of the karez was like a crater with a dark vein of water trickling soundlessly through it like blood. Walker adjusted the Barrett and AK-47 so that they hung below his chest when crawling on all fours. He turned to Bashir and embraced him. 'Borou bekheir, go with a blessing,' whispered the Afghan. Ferguson too hugged his friend of the last four weeks. There was a gentle splash as Walker stepped into the water, stooped into the darkness and then crawled into the tunnel. Then Bashir was alone beside the entrance, the huffing, puffing and splashing gradually ebbing away, leaving only a funereal silence beneath the starry sky. He shivered as the sweat cooled on his back.

All he had ever known since boyhood was war and despair. He had played his part against the Soviets as a messenger, though never a fighter. He had watched enviously as his older brothers – all three of them – went off to fight, and only one return, and he with a prosthetic limb. His father, having fled from his beloved museum in Kabul, had been so proud of them all, especially when the last Russian left. But as he grasped adulthood with hope in his heart, anarchy dashed his dreams of peace.

Then Walker had appeared, as if sent from God, to galvanise the local populace to reclaim the land from the blight of land mines. He had taught him so much by way of language, skills in medicine, and most of all by way of example. He had given them all desire to better themselves, where there had only been depression. In return Bashir had shown him the mountains, and beauty of Afghanistan; that was all that he could. He hated the Taliban, though they too were Pathans, for the war that they pursued against Massoud in the Panjsher and for the uneasy influence of the Arabs that leeched off them. *God, why couldn't they all just live in peace?* He was not unused to being on his own, in fact he preferred it; now bereft of his friend and leader he acutely felt the solitude and dread of the closing of their mission.

It was every bit as bad as Ferguson had feared; his comparatively huge frame had not been designed for such work, and his back began to ache at once, and his leg muscles became numb as they took the strain. Khalil scampered silently through the karez like a water rat behind Ferguson as Walker pushed on, drawing the former Sergeant with him like a shadow. Ferguson heard his own grunted exertions amplified in the small space between his ears and the tunnel sides; he felt Walker's soggy leather sandals in his face and their resultant splash, each step taking him closer to the quarter-mile openings. He gained comfort from each imprint on his forehead that he was not alone. '*You won't feel it after a quarter of a mile,*' Walker had said cheerfully back at Mushi. He gritted his teeth, hoping that in twenty minutes there would be a respite. '*This system is centuries old,*' he thought. '*It could collapse any minute*'...He felt his throat constrict, and forced the seeping paranoia from his mind.

Like three sociable moles they stood in the first opening. They were sunk into the ground, their limbs soaking, their backs creaking but above them was the purest starlight Ferguson had ever seen. He drank from his water bottle.

'Don't know why I bothered to bring this,' he complained.

'You'll need it when we get out of here,' said Walker, scanning the ground fore and aft with his night-sight from the limited viewpoint that he had in his trench.

'What's holding the ceiling up?'

'Some sort of clay cohesion I guess.'

'So not a lot then.'

'Don't worry – Khalil thinks that it's in pretty good nick,' replied Walker as the little Afghan stared serenely upwards at the stars, unable to understand their discourse. 'It's been here for donkeys' years, and besides, we got through the other day without mishap. He was telling me about the men that dug the karez years back. Apparently they formed a special caste, lived under special laws, ate special food, had extra rations. They died young as a rule…'

'You do surprise me,' said Ferguson, trying to pick out the North Star.

'Suffocation mostly. When they copped it all, their possessions and womenfolk went to the next karez man. Sons of karez men inherited the job, some were even branded at birth.'

'Like the bloody miners.'

'But once in the caste there was no escape; after a collapse or two, Khalil was saying the men would have to be driven back in with whips.'

'Just like the bloody miners.'

'Brutal stuff – but effective in its day. They're probably more akin to the Irish navvy than the miners though.' Walker wrapped his scope in its waterproof bag and stowed it in his knapsack. 'Are you fit?'

'Aye, I suppose so.' Walker ducked down into the tunnel again like a moorhen.

After the fifth of nine apertures and breaks, and nearly two hours of hard slog, Ferguson began to ease into the task, mentally seeing light at the end of the tunnel. He'd known from the start that three hours was ambitious with the stealth now required; after all, Khalil and Walker had no weapons to carry on their recce. They were nearing the sixth break point; he could sense the freshness of the air and an eagerness in Walker's pace, but suddenly Walker froze. He crashed into Walker's soles like a train in a shunting yard, squashing his nose.

Walker hadn't heard the noise above his own stertorous breathing. The first he had known of it was feeling the warm urine splattering off his sweaty head, running down his back and tumbling into the stream. He stopped, and desperately tried to control his breathing, but holding his breath made the blood pump in his ears and made it worse. A peel of laughter above him broke through his sonar. *'Were they laughing at him? Surely they didn't know that he was there – they couldn't see him, could they?'*

His eyes were salty with sweat; he turned his head sideways and slightly up. There was no torchlight. But there, quite distinct against the contrasting starlight to the total blackness of his previous thirty-minute journey, was a man. He saw the orange glow of a cigarette as the man sucked on it. He held it in an outstretched hand, which was received at the extreme edge of his peripheral vision by another. Two men. What the hell were they doing here? There had been too much dead ground in the open between the bridge and the hills, much of it filled with scrubby copses. From the last stop he hadn't been able to see all the ground above the line of the karez. This must be one of those scrubby patches, else surely he'd have seen the men before now.

Ferguson remained motionless, the cool water running beneath his arched body. Something was up, that's all he knew. He forgot his own pain. Then he saw the flare of a cigarette butt as it was tossed into the hole, momentarily throwing light into their watery grave. He heard it hiss, smelt the smoke caught in the slipstream above the water-line, and then felt the little butt nudge against his immersed left wrist as it drifted interminably on its own adventure. The man withdrew from the lip of the crater. Walker inched himself forward, and like a railway engine pulled Ferguson with him, cursing a missed station.

They did not stop at the next opening either.

It was two hours later that they reached the last mound, way behind their schedule. Walker popped his head above the parapet, gulping in the air whilst conscious of making as little noise as possible. Behind him, Ferguson controlled his desire to heave him out of the way. Patience and discipline were the watchwords, else all that backbreaking crawling would be in vain. They had no idea who their interlopers had been, nor indeed who and what lay in front or behind them. At last Walker leant down and gently tugged him into the night air, where he stretched his aching back gratefully as Walker continued to scan the hillside that rose above them like a menacing black tidal wave pulling in the surf before crashing down.

'Looks all clear behind,' murmured Walker to himself. 'Must have been those damned goat-herds.' The *nullah* was the last but one stage of their insertion and appeared free of visible signs of danger. He scanned the gully up as far as he could see to the first false summit, methodically covering the ground left and right to be as sure as he could that there were no listening posts. 'And all clear to the front.'

He took the Barrett and AK-47 from his body, heaved himself out of the hole, and carrying a weapon in each hand, doubled across the thirty yards of open country, crouching low, keeping to the shadows of the night. Ferguson gave him a minute and then followed, having helped Khalil up and watched him go ahead.

'It's straight up from here. Maybe nine hundred metres. I won't give a time estimate based on my last one,' Walker whispered.

'I'm glad of that.'

'I'll lead.' As he smiled, so his white teeth shone out of his stained face against the black night.

It was hard going underfoot in just sandals. They moved with assiduous care as though their lives depended upon it; every clanking rock was a personal failure and potential compromise. They cradled their rifles in one arm for balance, and Walker reverted to carrying the Barrett across his back. Initially the nullah was wide and flat with obvious obstacles, but as they ascended the sides became steeper, holding the darkness and the chill air like a shut fridge. Progress became slower as they fumbled around boulders of various shapes and sizes; their already soggy clothes became soaked with sweat. Walker stopped at every corner and summit where the nullah flattened out to spy the ground with his night sight, but only the stars seemed to watch over their advance. Then they reached the point of exit.

'We're here,' whispered Walker, having listened intently for any human activity. They were on a skyline in the saddle between the two hills. He took the Barrett from his back in order to soften his outline, and walked like an ape across the last two hundred yards to the OP, his bottom almost dragging on the floor. His thighs burned from the unusual exertion on the muscles as he moved silently forward. His arms hung low beside him and in each hand he held a weapon like a ski with which he gained an extra balancing hold; his body was upright, but hunched; his eyes and ears were alert for any alien movement. He stopped fifty yards short of the craggy outcrop from where he had looked down into the camp and made his sketches. He looked into it with his scope, looked again at the peaks, and then slithered into the coarse rocks like a reptile.

Their eyrie was a sandstone protrusion, like a crenellated forecastle. In it was a bed of tinder-dry, brittle sedge-like grass. He lay the Barrett beside him, pointing downhill – still in its case – whilst Ferguson swiftly erected the desert cam-net low across the top of the OP, securing the corners with a rock. The net sagged in the middle, mirroring the scoop in which the three men lay, the two Britons facing forward and Khalil to the rear.

'Nice 'n cosy,' whispered Ferguson. Walker was looking into the corrie and the valley below with his sight.

'You can see a couple of fires down there.' He heard an affirmative grunt. 'That'll be the cookhouse I guess. It's the permanent structure I showed you on the map.' Ferguson had his binoculars on the camp, the sky illuminating the scene little by little. He could see movement, like ants, black against a fuzzy background. They heard the faint echo of the azan carry to them.

'Reveille. We're just in time.'

'Morning prayers,' said Walker. 'They'll wash, pray a while, sit around reading the Qur'an and then breakfast.'

'We may as well get ours then.'

'Can you check the distance before that?' Ferguson took the laser from his knapsack and aimed it at the cookhouse.

'That's 955-metres. A longish shot.'

'Yeah, I thought as much. We've zeroed to nine hundred metres, and we know that it'll go twice that. The real skill – and luck – will be to get 'em together and take both out.'

'One would do I suppose.'

'We came for two,' Walker said emphatically. He retrieved a piece of naan bread from his knapsack and turned over his shoulder towards Khalil, whose eyes blinked slowly like a somnolent cat.

'You OK, old man?' asked Walker.

'Yes,' was the curt reply. Walker saw that he was knackered, the exertions finally telling on him.

'Try to eat something.' He motioned his naan to his mouth. 'It won't be long now. Rest your bones while you can.' Khalil smiled a weary smile, fighting off the tiredness. His eyes were heavy and salty. He rubbed his face, stretched an arm, and then pulled the wooden stock of his rifle into his shoulder and placed his cheek against it. He had to keep awake. They were depending upon his keeping a lookout to the rear. The honour of Kamir and Fazir Khan depended on him. He fell quietly asleep.

An hour later it was daylight. Walker had been right about the routine – men now sat around in huddles reading to each other. The air was still cool, their perch in shadow, and visibility at its zenith. The Barrett was out of its sleeve resting on its bi-pod, with Walker's sight fixed in place at the position he had scratched for it when zeroing. Both men scrutinised the camp through their telescopic sights. Ferguson counted thirty-one men distinctly, six of whom disappeared down the valley to the west on a run. No one had moved towards them.

'There's Sean Connor coming from the second tent in from the left in the row facing us,' said Walker, tightening his grip on the stock of the Barrett.

'Got 'im. Ugly bastard at this time of the morning.'

'Or any. Look at that battered face of his.' The Irishman had emerged wearing combat trousers and a navy-blue Hely-Hansen climbing top, holding his peach coloured towel and black wash-bag. 'Come on Murphy, you son of a bitch. Rise and shine.'

'Well lookee who's 'ere,' whispered Ferguson in surprise.

'Where? I don't see him?'

'Coming up from the right towards Connor. Fifty yards away. The mullah in the white robes.'

'Got him.'

'Abdul Qadir – top nob in al-Qa'eda. He's pretty thick with bin Laden.'

'Hmmm. Interesting little connection. I guess PIRA warrant such surety of handling.' Walker studied the face of the Arab for a moment in his scope, before settling his mark back on the Irishmen's tent. 'He has a dubious look about him, I'll give you that,' he muttered as much to himself as Ferguson. 'Come on Declan – get up you idle bastard.'

Ferguson was still looking at the Arab. 'He'd make a pretty good kill, don't you think?'

'Who… Oh, Qadir? I daresay, but we came for the paddies, not to turn the whole Islamic fundamentalist movement upside down… Oho… Who's coming from Connor's tent.' There was a hand from the inside gripping the flap.

'Listen, Piers, there's something that I need to tell you.'

'Yeah, what's that?' said Walker, taking aim at the tent opening beside which Connor stood looking up into the mountains, scratching under his arm and clearly talking to whomever was in the tent.

'Qadir…'

Ferguson never finished his sentence. The cam-net was ripped off the top of their hideout and four earnest looking Arabs pointed their AK-47s at them. A small man with pinched features and hollow black eyes, shouted in broken Dari:

'Drop weapons. Slowly. On knees.'

The two Britons complied, meekly followed by Khalil, awestruck and rubbing sleep and disbelief from his eyes. Terror and surprise were the competing emotions racing through the Britons as they looked at the small man. How had they been compromised? How had they missed the patrol? These were thoughts to be dealt with later. The present and how to deal with it was all that concerned them now.

'Holy fuck!' thought Ferguson. *'If – if, only I'd had the fucking gun, we'd have had 'em and be off by now for tea and medals.'* He struggled to control himself, not knowing what the excited jabbering of their captors meant, though he understood all too well the language of life and death pointed at him. It didn't look good. They couldn't fight back – that was clear. Should he continue with the part cast for him as a mute? He hoped that Piers would know what to do, would understand what was being said. After all, he had lived amongst them, and could read them – or so he bloody well hoped. All he could do was to follow his lead, and perhaps they would live.

The small man pulled a walkie-talkie from his hip and babbled excitedly into it in Arabic, of which Walker could pick up only that there was a vehicle waiting for them somewhere – and that meant reinforcements. Now, if ever, was the time to run. But where?

He saw from the corner of his eye that Khalil had advanced level with him. He turned his head sideways. The old man's eyes had narrowed with a determined, avenging intent. He moved his hand beneath his petou and struggled to free his bayonet from the rusted scabbard attached to his belt. His clenched fist was pumping away at the russet material, like a beating heart. Walker tried to prevent him, first with a look and then in Dari. A controlled three-round burst from the hip of one of the guards spun the taciturn old bodyguard, sending him tumbling face down to the ground.

'Place hands on heads,' said the small man in his pidgin Dari, the pupils of his brown eyes dilated with pleasure. They were rushed by two of the men and restrained brusquely in plasti-cuffs behind their backs.

'*Oh shit!*' thought Walker.

'Stand up,' the little man ordered, evidently relaxing into the situation. They were frisked as the small man came towards them, studying the Barrett rifle with interest. When he spoke into his walkie-talkie, Walker was certain that he had said 'Barrett'. This boded ill. The guy knew what they were on about, and any chance of bluffing seemed to fade. A voice at the other end barked instructions back.

Walker had heard enough, and recognising a change in the demeanour of the small man to one of insidious intent, realised that they were to be shot there and then, with questions asked later. Their disguises seemed to have stood up to silent interrogation, and so, acting on instinct, Walker lunged forward, prostrating himself on the ground like a seal. His brown beard was covered with dirt, cloying in his sweat. In Dari he implored the small man, who by now had his AK-47 levelled at his head:

'Don't shoot. We are British subjects. Not Afghans.'

Ferguson was fast losing the plot in what might as well have been a silent horror movie. On seeing his friend and comrade giving a good impression of an epileptic having a fit, he tensed himself in case it was a last desperate act of Walker's in which he was expected to join in. He stood his ground, little caring how or what he would have to do next – just that he would do it whatever the cost.

For the little Arab, this altered the situation – momentarily at least. He was flummoxed as he telegraphed this intelligence to the camp. The reply was curt and indecipherable. Walker looked up, his eyes wide with trepidation and pleading for mercy.

Most of the camp had gathered at the spent headwaters of the valley to see the two prisoners escorted in. There was a murmur as each man jostled for the best view, peeling off from the front of the queue like a rolling rugger-maul. One man pushed Ferguson to the ground, insulting him in Arabic. He stumbled, tripped and fell. His face was squashed onto a rock, which split the top of his cheek and blackened his eye. It swelled and tightened at once. The crowd laughed as he was manhandled to his feet. The small man was growing in stature as visibly as Ferguson's eye puffed out in cosmic colours; he shouted at the crowd to stand back and leave the prisoners alone. They fell back, following on in two lines like tassels on a kite.

'Phew! Will ya lok at dat piece o' hardware, Seany,' said Murphy over his shoulder. They had been watching through their tent flap as the Barrett was brought into the camp and paraded past them.

'De boys back home would give deir eye teeth to get another one of—' Connor stopped abruptly, and gripped Murphy's arm. 'De tall one – he ain't no Afghan, nor no Asiatic. An' de udder: take a look a' tim will ya?' They both studied the grubby, hirsute, and impassioned face as it passed. 'If I'm not mistaken, he could be de spittin' image of Captain Walker, late of de S-A-focken-S. De one dat did for us at de Silva Bridge.'

'Relax, Seany. You're paranoid. How de hell would dey be able to track us down to here. We didn't even know where we were coming to.' He patted Connor on the shoulder.

'An' how de hell did dey know we woz to be at de Silva Bridge dat night, eh, answer me dat? I tell ya, Dec, I never forget a face.' Connor's heart was pumping hard, and his face showed signs of exploding with fear as his mind tried vainly to subdue the illogical phobia taking over.

'An' even if it is dem Seany, I fancy twill be dey're last wakin' day. Dese bastards won't fock about with dem.' They tagged along with the procession.

Mustaffa, previously as adhesive as glue, now detached himself from the anxious pair. He moved like a ghost, outflanking the melee and appearing at the side of Abdul Qadir. He spoke confidentially into the ear bent towards him. A wry smile spread across Qadir's woolly mouth as he rested his right hand on the Czech-made CZ75 9mm fully automatic pistol at his side. In his left hand, Qadir carried a walkie-talkie.

Like Caesar, Qadir raised his right hand, and the advancing men stopped in front of him and dispersed into a circle around himself, the Britons and the patrol.

'Who are you?' asked Qadir quietly in English.

'I told you dey were Brits, Dec,' muttered Connor under his breath, watching from the wings.

The two captives stood with their heads bowed, Ferguson content to let the other lead. Though their prospects looked as bleak as they had perhaps ever known, Walker would, if he could, find a way out for them.

'We are British citizens,' replied Walker calmly and with politeness, but now looking solidly into the dark eyes of Qadir.

'Citizens? Huh!' retorted the Arab contemptuously but without raising his voice any higher. He was in control. 'And what would citizens be doing with a highly powerful sniping rifle looking into my little camping excursion?'

Walker had received plenty of time to think about how he might handle every situation that arose from this confrontation. They had decided way back in the Borders that at all costs they would not implicate the British Government. This was their own damn fool caper, and their own damn fault if caught, no matter how betrayed they felt by the actions of their own government.

'You've two Irishmen in your camp.' The Arab raised a black eyebrow. 'We came to kill them.' The Arab began to smile. 'They killed a friend of ours.' The Arab laughed out loud.

'I don't focken believe dis,' exclaimed Connor, the veins in his neck bulging, his face contorted with rage. It was outlandish – too far out of scope for his mind to get a hold of. Murphy tried in vain to hold him back as he propelled himself into the circle and stood behind Qadir's shoulder. Murphy moved cautiously to his side, eyeing Walker as though he were a dangerous animal.

'Always the coward, eh Seany,' said Walker.

'Dey're Brit soldiers, Qadir. Focken SAS soldiers. What are ya waitin' for? Kill dem! Kill dem!' he shrieked. Qadir half turned towards him with the faintest of amused smiles curling his whiskered lips.

'We are not British soldiers,' Walker replied defiantly, his eyes never faltering from holding Qadir's. 'We came here for retribution. Your guests murdered our friend. That's all. We caught them once, when – yes – we were soldiers, but our government saw fit to release them. We came here on our own to kill them.'

Qadir drew his pistol. He inspected it, as if checking for imperfections, whilst Connor implored him to kill the Britons. Murphy gently tried to quell his invective. Qadir gripped the pistol tightly in his right hand, bringing it up to head height in a smooth action and in slow motion extended his arm. The two men were no more than six-feet away. He swung his arm round and in the same movement depressed the trigger.

The bullets entered his neck, then rose up the side of his head as the gun reared from the five-round burst of automatic fire. Bright red blood squirted out as his throat was severed, and a squeaky noise whistled haltingly and then fell silent as his last breath escaped. Connor reeled and jerked from the impact. He clutched Murphy's arm as he slumped to the ground, his blood congealing, tar-like, with the fine white dust of the valley's floor. His legs kicked twice and then were still.

Murphy's face was ashen with shock as he tried to pull his friend from him in a desperate attempt to escape the psychotic gunman that Qadir had turned into. A sense of outrage and uselessness took over as he knelt beside Connor and looked up with bloodshot eyes into the cold, sneering face of Qadir.

'You bastard! You mad, focken bastard!'

'On the contrary; you are the bastard. You have shown us nothing but contempt since you began this mismatched misadventure, and now – now you draw these foreigners into our intrigue.' He jerked his head towards Walker, took aim at Murphy's head and fired off the rest of the magazine. The body writhed on the ground, felled by the first round and then twitched no more.

Ferguson and Walker looked on with the confused satisfaction of having witnessed their work done for them, but also with asphyxiating anxiety. And yet through this entire visceral spectacle, Walker whimsically determined some hope, even in the hands of the deranged Arab. Their ears rang, and the smell of copper and gunpowder, so natural to them, now turned the pit of their stomachs. Ferguson bent forward and retched.

A white Toyota pick-up charged up the valley from the west, leaving a burgeoning cloud of dust in its wake. The driver was hooting his horn continuously, whilst the half-dozen men in the back waved their arms in the air, firing off AK-47s wildly into the echoing hills. As they drew nearer they heard the exultant cries of:

'Allah Akbar! Allah Akbar!'

A lithe-looking Afghan in a white pyjama suit and open sandals jumped from the moving cab and ran towards the scene of the executions. The man was carrying his rifle in his right hand, parallel to the ground; his left held his flowing white turban to his head. He spoke rapidly in Dari to Qadir, mindless of what had just occurred, gulping in air as he swallowed his words:

'Ahmed... Massoud... dead... assassinated... yesterday... in... the... Panjsher.'

The crowd surrounding the two shell-shocked Brits danced with joy, wailing and screaming like dervishes until their lungs could take no more. Rifles were fired into the air saluting the rapturous news. At their feet a cloud of flies gathered over the two corpses, the more adventurous of which were already settling on the warm wounds and rivulets of blood of their own joyous feast. It was the 10th of September 2001.

Chapter 13

Hereford, 13 September 2001

As Robert Ross entered the troop office, Sergeant Jimmy Rothwell sprung to his feet, discarding the Daily Star on the desk.

'Wha's the news, boss?'

'We're off in two hours time. Get the boys together in an hour for a briefing. Everyone should be ready to go.'

'Aye boss, they are that.' Jimmy's eyes sparkled with excitement.

'Right then, I'll see you in the War Room in an hour.' Jimmy grabbed his beret and walked purposefully out of the door, leaving his troop commander pondering over a map of Afghanistan pinned to the wall.

Robert Ross was a big man – six-feet and three-inches – with two hundred pounds packed around a solid frame. From the age of five all he had ever wanted to do was to wear the kilt of his father's and grandfather's now amalgamated regiment, the Queen's Own Highlanders, and on attaining that goal at the age of nineteen he had only dreamt of being in the SAS, a goal he had pursued with single-minded intent. Now at the age of thirty, he was about to be dropped into Afghanistan with his troop of sixteen men on a top-secret mission. Ostensibly it was a forward reconnaissance operation in the Hindu Kush – intelligence gathering, assessing the strength of and establishing links with anti-Taliban forces. That is what they would do, and that is what he would tell his troop.

His father had retired from the army as a young captain, having extended his National Service. He had then joined the Diplomatic

Service from which he had been posted to Islamabad where he had made a name for himself after Partition. He had married late and Robert, their only son, had been born and brought up in Pakistan until he was fifteen, when at last his father had retired to the east coast of Scotland.

Robert had a gift for Asiatic languages, speaking Urdu like a native, Dari fluently and tolerably good Arabic, which in the Gulf War he had been called upon to deploy as a liaison officer with his regiment. He had passed SAS selection at the first attempt, and proved himself an able officer in counter-terrorism work in Ulster. Having earned his spurs he had been loaned to the Sultan of Oman for a short training period of three months from where he had recently returned. He was an obvious choice for the mission. Rothwell was not. There was no doubting his aptitude, proven beyond question over six years service with G-Squadron, but he had baggage – baggage he didn't know he had.

*

Ross observed the two rows of tents in the putative al-Qa'eda training camp half a kilometre below him. For the twenty-four hours since being deployed, he had established a ring of OPs around the head of the valley. Their intelligence appeared to have been good, but their deployment too late. The tents leant awry, battered by a channelled wind that had folded two of them. A twist of dust danced in front of the long, low adobe serai, the camp's only permanent structure. Through his binoculars he watched as Jimmy Rothwell's team crept stealthily along the spur just above this serai.

'Nice 'n easy now,' he mumbled to himself as he saw Corporal Jessops break cover and advance through the encampment. The team, operating in pairs, silently cleared each tent in turn. Ross saw Jessops and one of the troopers – he couldn't quite make out who it was – converge in the open space between the tents and the building, like batsmen discussing the state of the wicket between overs. Jessops waved three times from his left shoulder to his right.

'Tommy, you stay here with your boys,' he said, looking over his shoulder, 'and cover our rear.'

'Right boss,' grinned Toms. 'Stay here till you call us down, eh?'

'That's it.' He raised himself from his prone position, as did a patrol of four SAS-men and his signaller and runner, who now followed a serpentine route into the camp.

That the camp had been broken in a hurry was evidenced in the cookhouse where pots of yellowed, hardened rice had been left with ladles cemented into them. In black-iron cauldrons a desiccated stew looked like bones protruding through a tight rubber film. Around these, swarms of black flies performed aerobatic displays. Outside, fossilising turds gave off a malodorous stench that mingled with the concentrated smell of urine in an area devoid of air currents.

'*Animals*,' thought Ross.

The silent precision of the operation was rudely broken by hoarse Arabic cries from somewhere set off from the tented area, sending the soldiers diving for cover. The cries stopped at once, only to sound again, this time with more desperation.

'Do you see anything?' shouted Ross to Jessops, who was nearer to the sound.

'Aye, boss. There's some sort of cave over there. It's barricaded and there seems to be a youngish-looking local trying to draw our attention,' returned the corporal, studying the ground with his binoculars.

'Take a look, will you.' Ross saw the four men move off towards a rocky buttress on the far side of the valley, covering each other as they manoeuvred. There followed a short burst from a G-3 and then he saw a young Afghan boy being helped from the barred cave. The boy blinked in the sunlight as he emerged, emaciated and pale faced.

'He says he was locked up for missing prayers,' said Ross to Jessops. 'The Arabs, he says, left him here to die many days ago. Says we've saved his life.' Jessops looked at the boy without feeling.

Ross lifted the boy's weak fluffy chin with his left hand and looked sternly into his eyes – don't mess with me was the signal strongly conveyed.

'The ferangis,' stammered the boy, trying to break from his stare, 'they... in the head.' He tried to raise two fingers to his temple only to meekly drop his hand as a weapon was drawn up into his stomach.

'Where are they now?'

'Dead.' The boy looked timidly away, to indicate either the scene or its horror. 'Shot.' Ross dropped the boy's chin, which slumped to his chest.

'Are they buried here?' asked Ross, sympathetically now.

'Yes – I think so. And then they left.'

'The graves – where are they?'

'I do not know. I heard the shots and saw a crowd on the other side of the valley.' The boy pointed.

He was led to the far side where the hard grey earth was littered with myriad empty cases from assorted pistols and rifles. Three heavy machine-gun pits had been etched out and were brimming over with spent brass. Beneath the pockmarked edifice where the targets had been set up, Ross spotted two fresh graves parallel to the slope. There was no marker, simply the dried earth and rocks piled on top of what lay below.

The bodies were dusty white with blood caked on their horribly disfigured faces and torsos like tar. They had been interred on their sides facing a small niche, a qibba, carved into the wall of the grave facing in the direction of Mecca. A jute rag had been used to tie up their mouths and it made them look like escaped lunatics. The eyes were closed. White linen ends had been stuffed into their mouths, and dripped from them like saliva. Ross bent beside each cadaver with a sense of bewilderment. *Who were these foreigners?* He turned to the boy.

'How did this happen?' asked Ross, wearily.

'Two Afghans were caught snooping in the hills above the camp. There was much excitement. Then the Arabs shot the ferangi. That's all I know.' The boy was crying.

'Do you know who they were?' asked Ross, pointing his weapon at the bodies.

'One called Mister Sean, and other, Mister Declan.' The SAS Captain loosened perceptibly.

Chapter 14

The cellar was dank and fetid, with only a thin rectangular slit at the top pricking the gloom ten feet below. It singularly failed to move the acrid stench of urine and excrement. The walls were of a cracked whitewash, discoloured by great sweeps and handprints of the living paint of its previous occupants. The room was bare of furnishings save for the twelve rusting iron rings fixed to the walls, three on each of the four sides, positioned at the tidemark of blistered paint-work caused by the seeping damp. The door was made of battered steel with a square aperture cut into it at head height, barred with a grill. Beyond it sat two Arab guards on three-legged wooden stools; a table stood between them with half-drunk grubby glasses of chai and AK-47s leaning against it. Their task was to keep a round-the-clock vigil on the pile of sweat and blood stained rags, caked in human faeces that was heaped in one corner of the cellar.

The stamp of feet was heard coming from above with concomitant flip-flopping, shuffling and groaning noises. One of the guards stood up, jangled a set of keys in the cellar door and pushed it stiffly back. No one spoke as the stooped, bedraggled figure of Ferguson was rudely pressed into the room and forced down against the wall opposite. The escort chained his limp, manacled wrists to the ring, and then padlocked the chain. Pestilent juices wept from their suppurating wounds. As the escort left, the guard slammed the door shut and turned the key.

The heap in the corner stirred. Through this septic womb, Walker looked across the room, pushing his battered legs out from his adopted foetal position. His face was lacerated from his right ear to his chin, badly bruised and swollen, but still he forced a painful smile at his comrade. Ferguson nodded faintly, wincing as he did.

They had been taken from Navor the same morning they were accosted, arriving in Kabul six hours later, and deposited in the dungeon in which they had languished for the past two days. Their glimpse of Kabul had been brief and only from the back of Qadir's Land Cruiser, with its blacked-out windows. It hadn't changed perceptibly since Walker had last been there, though the derelicts looked more derelict if that were possible, and the faces of the people longer – perhaps drained of their souls. Yet there seemed to be order, and above all peace – people no longer scurried from house to house – and gone were the competing and constant artillery barrages. The market stalls had maintained their colour and there was still a Kabuli energy evident about their vendors. Taliban patrols walked with languid, authoritative strides. He had caught glimpses of flashing smiles from some of the sentry posts, noting an exultant glee about them in contrast to the pedestrians cowed under burqa and sharia law. Of course they had much to be happy about if the news was true. Massoud had been the Taliban's only credible threat, and now his last stronghold in Afghanistan must surely be at the Taliban's mercy.

An hour later the escort returned, this time to claim Walker from the cell.

The interrogation block was a short drive away, perhaps only five minutes. Inside the plain white cell there were two wooden chairs, an old school desk, a heavy metal door with a single keyhole and no handle, a 100-Watt bulb shone brightly from a six-inch flex in the centre of the ceiling, and beside it a meat-hook hung from a thick, grubby white rope. Beneath the hook was a sticky puddle of blood, and bloody footprints. Above the door, inscribed in Pashtu was the motif: '*Throw reason to the dogs. It stinks of corruption*'.

The four guards who filled the room – two at the door and two behind his chair – changed with every session. His interrogator was a weedy looking Arab, with broken features hidden behind a black sheen of grizzled beard that had failed to sprout over the rivulets of scar tissue. He had a frightful squint in his left eye, and a withered left arm. He never changed. Nor did his evil manner and addiction to tobacco, an oddity for a devout Wahhabist such as Walker presumed him to be. The ashtray on the desk, beside his lined-paper notebook and pencil, overflowed with stubs.

Walker was pushed into a seat and the bag pulled from his head. His inquisitor looked up, as if welcoming an old friend to his table, then stood, barely extending his height over the seated Scot by two inches. His weak, angular frame was shrouded in a voluminous beige shalwar shameez. He stared quizzically at Walker for a short while before issuing his opening gambit in a soft, hissing tone, 'So, Mister Walker – you have nothing to say for yourself?'

Walker stared fixedly at him. *'Go on, do your worst, you pathetic brown weasel of humanity. Let's get this over with,'* he thought. The Arab looked up at the two men behind the chair and nodded. The chair was abruptly pulled back and Walker dragged to his feet. His arms were extended and a bloodied rope tied round his manacled hands, before the other end was thrown over the meat hook. Walker tensed himself as the two guards heaved on the rope until he was on tiptoe, almost hanging like a carcass, and the steel fetters bit the putrid wounds around his wrists. He allowed himself a strained grimace. One of the men lifted the tail of his shirt and tossed it over his matted head, exposing the still-weeping wounds of previous visitations.

'You know the form by now,' said the Arab. 'We beat you till you drop; we enjoy ourselves. You can't take any more, pass out, and are returned to your friend. So tedious. So... come on, why not give yourself a break and tell us who sent you here, and how you knew where and who we are, eh?' The man played lazily with his worry beads.

Walker couldn't grit his teeth because his jaw was fractured. He focused on a cockroach scuttling between his feet. The first lash of the three-foot wire antenna stripped of its plastic coating whipped across his back, hungrily gorging the ruptured skin. He choked on the wind he sucked desperately inwards, spluttering blood-flecked spittle across the room. '*You bastards!*' he cried inwardly. '*You cowardly, pathetic, bastards!*' Another lash had the Arab, now seated, perversely grinning with wicked excitement. '*God! He probably gets a hard-on from this sordid little spectacle.*'

'Come on, Piers, let's break this monotonous cycle, shall we. Barry has already confirmed that it was the Ishmaelis who supported you, and that you are on a US sponsored assassination attempt of our operatives.' Walker had nothing to lose but his life, and he couldn't save himself. He couldn't even save himself from himself. But he must at all costs not implicate his friend, the good Kamir, and though it seemed inevitable that he would become a PR pawn, he must hold out from drawing his quest into a national vendetta.

He had been right at the outset; they were insane to imagine that they could get away with it. His immature machismo had urged one last demonstration of virility and independence of mind. They had witnessed the deaths of Connor and Murphy – what they had come to do, but they had lost what they had come with – their integrity and their lives. And they hadn't changed anything... had they? But in death, as in life, he knew that he was right. The rule of the bully must be snuffed out wherever it is found – the IRA, the Islamic, African and, indeed, Western tyrannies, as much as the school bully. He was a martyr to his cause, even if no one else knew that he was, nor even that he had such a cause. He dug deep into his soul, his past training and his principles. He remembered an old hymn:

> *Dear Lord and Father of mankind,*
> *Forgive our foolish ways...*

How appropriate, but more so the last verse:

Breathe through the heats of our desire
Thy coolness and Thy balm;
Let sense be dumb, let flesh retire;
Speak through the earthquake wind and fire,
O still small voice of calm.

Another lash cut more stingingly into his shoulders, and then quickly and petulantly across his backside and thighs. '*That must have excited old bone-face!*' But he was fading. The routine of two days had drained him. He shat himself involuntarily – a watery, putrid excrement trickling down the inside of his thighs and tingling his wounds. Like an old hand at midwifery, the Arab had seen it all before and did not flinch.

Now the Arab stood before him, yanking at his scrawny beard, shaking Walker's head from side to side. His eyes had misted over; lucid thought fast ebbing from him. His mind was circling – thoughts chasing thoughts. The Arab drew on his cigarette. 'One last time: who sent you?' Walker closed his eyes, and then snapped them open. He sensed the heat, smelt the tobacco smoke. The Arab, with a macabre toothy grin, held the butt between the forefinger and thumb of his right hand and stubbed it out on Walker's cheek. The smell of his singed beard caught in his nostrils, and then the searing pain penetrated his all but numbed feelings. He slumped limply in his hanging position like a puppet.

The third morning witnessed a sea change. Neither man was taken away, whilst the guards, instead of sitting in stoical silence, chatted amongst themselves with great excitement. A hard-boiled egg was given to each man for breakfast with bowls of curds and a portion of naan bread. Though training had wised the former SAS soldiers to such an obvious tactic, nonetheless they accepted the food gratefully.

Since they had arrived, the food had been a miserly Afghan stew of bones and scraps of meat mixed with boiled rice that had to be force-fed to them by their unsympathetic guards. They had swallowed what they could without choking. It had become a routine which the guards found a source of great merriment, as much as children enjoy watching feeding time at the zoo.

Now the guards seemed to be finding their amusement elsewhere. They changed as usual before lunch, Afghans replacing Arabs, and still the beatings were not resumed. Walker heard them cackling like witches about the 'Great Satan' and 'his towers of evil being destroyed'. The men had laughed, and then one of them had made the noise of an aeroplane. Intrigued and strengthened by the extended respite and nourishment of solid food, Walker bum-shuffled to the keyhole of the door and peered through it.

The guards were young men of perhaps nineteen, and the one making the aeroplane noises had his arms extended like a high-wire circus act. The other stood on his stool shaking with giggles as his friend flew at him, knocking him to the ground. The guard picked himself up and stood on the other stool, laughing more uproariously now as the 'aeroplane' collided with him, again shying him from his perch. 'Allah Akbar! Allah Akbar!' they cried with one voice. Walker thought that they were mere children playing in a frightening adult world and pitied them for their harsh, pathetic prospects in life.

Still the beatings held off. When at last the door was opened again, four Afghans appeared with two buckets of warm water, two towels and fresh clothes. '*That old chestnut,*' thought the doubting Ferguson bitterly. Their clothes were cut from them as they sat, still chained to the wall, and their wounds attended to carefully with the warm water. Further buckets were produced and at last a feeling of cleanliness returned. Hard cheese and naan were given to them for lunch.

An hour later the weedy interrogator returned with two armed guards. The Britons looked at him with stoical faces. The guards collected around Walker, and pulled him gently to his feet. They unchained him from the wall, undid his handcuffs and then re-applied them behind his back.

'Please, after you, Mr Walker,' said the man sycophantically.

*

It was a perfect cloudless autumnal day in Kabul; a light warm breeze wafted across the dusty rose garden.

'Afghans love their flowers. Extraordinary, don't you think, Mr Walker?' said Abdul Qadir, smiling kindly. Walker said nothing. He found himself with his enslaver at one end of a walled garden enclosure – a rose garden quartered by a shingle path and neat box hedging. At either end were arched wrought iron gates with vertical bars and a sliding latch, beside which stood two impressively pantalooned Afghan guards with rifles strapped across their chests. Two more guards shadowed their slow shuffling advance from one end to the other, and two more mirrored them along the pathways parallel to the central one.

'You enjoyed your meal last night, I hope?' The Arab's eyes twinkled mischievously, and were again met with silence from his companion. 'A bit of a rarity in these parts, you know.' They walked slowly on, Qadir allowing for his discomfort. 'I imagined them to be quite tough so I had the cook batter them with a rifle butt for you.'

'What are you talking about?'

'Balls – tasty were they?'

'What?' he replied indifferently.

'Well, I mean, their former owner won't be needing them anymore!'

'You what!' cried Walker disgustedly.

'You see we knew it was the Ishmaelis who had helped you.' At this he tapped the side of his semitic nose. 'We just had to catch one of them, and do you know what?' Walker didn't answer; his mind was in a blur. 'He told us that in fact you were only after the Irishmen after all.' He laughed sardonically.

'You utter bastard.'

'Funny – wasn't that what Mr Murphy said before I killed him?' retorted Qadir tartly. 'But no matter, now that we have cleared that little mystery you will perhaps be of some collateral and propaganda importance to us now. You see it has begun, Mr Walker.'

'What has begun? The death of Massoud? Others will take his place. The country is untenable from central governance.'

'Exactly,' said Qadir, smiling as if winning some unseen point of argument. 'You have perchance heard of our other minor success?' He raised a quizzical eyebrow. 'No? It is nothing – as I say, just the beginning.' He walked on, then paused to cup an apricot bloom in his hand before turning to Walker. 'Two days ago the glorious shadid destroyed the World Trade Centre in New York.' Walker's jaw dropped. He knew damn well that it had long been the target of Islamic fundamentalists. 'They hijacked two of your own jumbo jets and flew them into the twin towers, which tumbled like a house of cards.'

It seemed too incredible that in the land of civilisation and plenty such an act could take place. It didn't seem possible – here, of course, but there, no way. He remembered the childish antics of his guards earlier that day and his pity for them turned to bile in his stomach.

'How many killed?' he asked meekly.

'Many thousands. They are still counting what they can find.'

'You'll never get away with it.'

'Indeed?' said Qadir, almost willing reprisals.

'Innocent lives just rubbed out. That's not the way of Allah.'

'Come now, Mr Walker – innocent? I don't agree. And distaste for what we have perpetrated – how can you judge, when you have travelled thousands of miles to exact revenge on two men?'

'But they were guilty of murdering and maiming. They were bad men. Criminals. Terrorists. And we only wanted to kill them.'

'Psht! And how many others have been killed along the way? No Mr Walker, I can agree with you perhaps only in terms of scale. Revenge is revenge, and some circumstances require desperate measures to uphold what you believe in. You and I, we are more similar than you might imagine. In fact, I rather admire you and Mr Ferguson.'

'But you can't just go around attacking other countries.'

'Really? Isn't that how Britain became "Great"? You see, Mr Walker, when your way of life is threatened you must act. And if that threat is corrosive secular influences – how did your Mr Orwell put it? – um – *carnivorous capitalism* – then we must strike at its lifeblood – take out the heart of capitalism.'

'They'll rebuild. A mere pinprick in historical terms.'

'Of course, of course,' conceded Qadir. 'It is a symbol. But it is the beginning, as I say.'

'You can never hope to sustain your attack... you can't possibly think that you can defeat a global system, a whole culture, and let alone America. You cannot win this.'

'And you? You've already lost.' He walked slowly on again, and stopped at the crossing of the pathways contemplating which way to go. He went straight on. 'Your culture is dying before your eyes but you're too dazzled by opulence and opportunity to see it.'

'And yours? What is it if not backward, repressive – feudal even?'

'Indeed? But it is strong; it is binding; it is guiding both spiritually and morally. Your Church of England is corrupt – it doesn't even believe in God. It is just a freak show in a circus. Its leaders are sponsored by chocolate companies – Cadbury and Yorkie.'

'Cantebury and York,' interjected Walker, not believing the naivety of the man.

'Whatever. And its mainstays have no religious connotation at all. Christmas is a consumerist sacrifice on an altar of self-interest. Easter is a corporate event hijacked by global confectionery companies.'

'Surely you can't be anti-capitalist?'

'On the contrary. Have you read Qutb?'

'No.'

'Pity – you should, you know. Your brand of capitalism is corrupt… your Mr Kipling put it rather well:

> *'There are four good legs to my father's chair,*
> *People and Priests, Land and Crown…'*

Walker completed the couplet.

> *'…I sits on all of them fair and square*
> *And that's the reason it don't break down.'*

'Bravo,' said Qadir with surprise. 'You see we have more in common than you thought already.'

Walker looked at the Arab with indifference and condescendingly replied, 'I congratulate you on your knowledge of Kipling.'

Qadir was obviously gratified. 'It is important to know the imperialist sentiments of one's oppressor, don't you think? And it serves to illustrate my point. You see, in the West, and by that I mean the British started it, you have put between yourselves and your God your own institutional gods, and then you have systematically chipped away at them. To have done so in my eyes, precisely demonstrates the moribund core of your values. And what is more it must be stopped before it pervades Islamic regions, appealing to the baser whims of mankind. We are, after all is said and done, of one flesh.'

'But you can't stop it. You can't even hide yourself away from it.'

'We shall see.'

'It is the way of history, of life itself. To stop is to die. To change, to morph, is to grow. Civilisations, cultures, they continually evolve. You can't hold on. You must adapt.'

'But if to adapt is to compromise what you believe in, then you are left with a humanist creation that is corrupt in its soul. The injil, the Gospels, tell you as much do they not? You must stand up for what you cherish and hold to be true, and to die in so doing is honourable. Believe me, Mr Walker – we are right and you are wrong.'

They ambled on, flanked by dusty blooms throwing up sweet perfumes reminding Walker of the small comforts of life that seemed to have been denied to him now for eternity. From the perspective of the stalking militiamen it was obvious that the two men were engaged in a respectful battle, each vying for the position of tutor to student.

'Take the Taliban,' continued Walker. 'They took over Afghanistan and are now changing it to their ways. So be it.'

'That's not how your governments view them though is it?'

'Lives, people, cultures, civilisations – you name it. They are all just footprints on a beach. And perhaps you're right, that right now the herd instinct means they're all wearing Nike trainers. But they will all be washed away by the tides of time. The sea remains a constant, and the sand too; a beach upon which new imprints will be made. Some of these become merged, and some are so deep and coloured in such a fashion that they take time to wash out – but they go in the end.'

'You seem to think that it will be our ways that go. Why not yours?'

'I don't at all. But you will be hunted down and smashed – of that I am sure. Islam? No. We are mature enough as a world to respect each other, are we not?' Qadir was clearly tickled by this and chuckled out loud.

'Hubris will be the undoing of you, Mr Walker. Of course the Americans will come. They'll bounce the rubble in this fly-infested country with their mighty armaments. The Taliban? Oh, they'll capitulate as Afghans habitually do against conventional odds. Al-Qa'eda will disperse like smoke – it already has. A great American victory will be lauded: a symbol of their might. A puppet regime will be imposed; grand promises made; gestures even – but all vacuous.' Qadir was enjoying himself. 'To rebuild this country will take billions of dollars, vision and commitment. Do you have that?' he challenged. 'The regime will crumble in time – slowly perhaps, but it will. Secular values will be put upon the people like Armani suits – incongruous and without understanding. A jihad will be called…'

'You mean the one that bin Laden advocates isn't real?'

'Of course it is.'

'Come on, you know as well as I do that he doesn't have the religious standing to invoke a jihad.'

'He is endorsed by the mullahs.'

'This is a one-man – a very rich man, granted – crusade against the West.'

'Not a good choice of words,' cut in the Arab. 'If I may conclude? The West will be faced with a stark choice. To commit in strength – economic, political, and military – to rebuild Afghanistan despite the better instincts of its people, a people by then in arms and defiance against them? Or to retreat in ignominy as the Russians before them. As I said, we must attack the lifeblood, and we will bleed you dry:

> *'When you're wounded and left on Afghanistan's plains*
> *And the women come out to cut up what remains*
> *Just roll to your rifle and blow out your brains*
> *An' go to your Gawd like a soldier.*

'Kipling again,' said Qadir with satisfaction.

Walker felt the weight of logic and history upon him. It had happened to the British twice before, and then in modern times to the Russians; indeed their Afghan misadventure had precipitated the unravelling of the Communist ideology. His head hurt from injuries sustained by his inquisitors and from the bright sunlight. He shuffled to a halt.

'But they'll get you. And they'll get bin Laden.'

'Like you said about Massoud, *'There will be others in his place'*; and besides, I don't think it likely that they'll get us all, do you? And if that is my qismet, then I am ready to die the death of a shahid.' They were near to one of the exits. 'And then there will be Iraq, Saudi Arabia, Palestine. You are about to witness the nemesis of Western hegemony – attacked and terrorised at home; attacking abroad, only to be attacked and terrorised. As you say, Mr Walker, *'To stand still is to die'*.' He stopped to watch a bee collecting pollen from a beautiful fragrant pink rose; an irenic smile puckered his beard as his pupils dilated, his eyes moistened, and then like a wicked, irascible schoolboy he flicked the bee violently away. The bloom crumbled and its petals parachuted to the ground. Qadir's eyes narrowed, squeezing a teardrop from each, at once lost in his black whiskers. He forced a smile at Walker. 'I have enjoyed our little chat. We shall meet again very soon, Insha'Allah.' The sleek Arab bowed courteously and passed through the gate held open for him. Two guards ushered Walker back the way he had come with the barrels of their rifles probing his tender wounds.

*

Ferguson sat hunched against the damp wall, his head lolling in the saddle between his bony, aching knees. His mind was wandering between the dread of further interrogation and the guilt that he bore heavily within his soul. The guilt of deceit, of shamming the one person he had come to revere as much as his dear father. His spirits were weakening, as low as they had ever been. He'd never faced capture and interrogation before, save during SAS Selection – and that seemed a breeze by comparison. He wouldn't buckle – he couldn't. The Taliban could make PR hay out of it of course through invention, but not through his own collusion. He wished it were all over. He wanted to tell Walker, if only to assuage some of his conscience – but he couldn't. He couldn't bear to look him in the eye and tell him that he'd lied. He owed it to him not to implicate him any further than he had. Their story was a good one. It stood up to scrutiny, but only if he kept it to himself.

Slowly he raised himself as the door to the cell was unlocked and Walker returned, only this time shackled to the wall beside him. Ferguson shifted with considerable pain to make way for him, when in fact there was no need. He looked at the guards distrustfully, but they didn't return his wistful, glazed look. New tactics – the softly-softly approach meant new dangers. Once the guards had left the room, he whispered through his beard:

'How did it go – you don't look too bad?'

'Had a quiet chat with the Arab. It was surreal. He took me to some rose garden for a walk, and then he told me that they'd blown up the World Trade Center in New York.'

'They did what!'

'Shhh. Easy. Apparently just hijacked a couple of jumbos and flew them into the towers. Collapsed in a heap.'

'Bloody hell.'

'He thinks this will be the beginning of the end of the West's influence on the world.'

There was silence for a while as each mulled over this staggering turn of events. Somehow the atrocity changed things for Ferguson; he was no longer harbouring a burden of guilt. His deception seemed to have found an end. He steeled himself to speak to Walker.

'Hey listen, Piers, I'm sorry that I ever got you involved in all of this…'

'Hey, don't worry. I was as much up for it as you were. Besides, we got what we came for, just not quite how we'd planned it. Anyway I reckon that we've seen the worst of the ill-treatment for now.' He paused to control his emotions. He didn't want to waste the opportunity to impart what little he had gleaned, not knowing how long they might have together. 'By *'for now'*, I mean just that. They'll play some devious PR game with us and the world – he said as much. We're some sort of collateral, dead or alive it makes no difference to them.'

'Back there when we were blown...' Ferguson turned the conversation back.

'What of it?'

'I was gonna tell you then – I had to.' He looked sideways at his friend from the corner of his blackened left eye. 'Qadir – well he's an important guy to al-Qa'eda...'

'Yeah, so you said before.'

'He's got some early influence on bin Laden. Their families come from the same shite-hole in the Yemen – al-Rubat in Hadramawt. That sort thing matters to bin Laden – like the old school tie. They went to uni together in Jeddah – that's where they first met.' He was fumbling for his words, short of breath and racked by the inner dread of a confessor. 'He introduced him to the Muslim Brotherhood – a bunch of Islamic crackpots.' He stopped.

'So what? He's a big cheese.'

Ferguson breathed deeply, though it hurt his chest. 'I didn't come here for Connor and Murphy – as much as I'm glad that they're gone. I came for Qadir.'

Walker was stunned. He looked up and stared into his old comrade's eyes. Ferguson went on. 'Qadir headed up the African al-Qa'eda team that blew the embassies. The Yanks knew it was him but they couldn't catch him to pin it on. So the Yanks and us put out a hit on him.'

'But I thought you'd left the regiment?'

'The DSF, Franklin – you remember him?'

'That ginger haired toe-rag?'

'It was part of my cover once they'd established a plan.'

Walker worked fast round the plot. 'You mean they released Connor and Murphy so they could get you to get me to do their dirty work? Surely someone else could have done this just as well.' He was angry, spitting through his whiskers.

'No one knew the language or the culture like you. No one had the connections you had on the ground. Since the Cold War ended everyone's forgotten about Afghanistan – that's why we're in this mess now. There was no human intelligence.'

'Un-fucking-believable!'

'But for what it's worth I don't reckon that they're that crooked. I mean how could they have engineered the PIRA/al-Qa'eda link, huh?' Walker partially withdrew his bristles. 'No, my take is that they knew PIRA was keen and that Qadir would be the guy most likely to handle it. The Irish sources gave them the pieces; they put it together and then worked back from there to us. Simple. Then they needed to cover all bases in case of compromise.'

'It just worked out that way, eh?' said Walker slowly and solemnly. He sank his head between his knees and closed his eyes. He'd been used. He thought of home: his father, the factory buzz, of Jenny... In all probability he'd lose her, even were he by some miracle to retain his life. She'd go home – probably already had – thinking him a bastard, not understanding why or where he'd gone; all trust broken down. His dreams had been destroyed by the machinations of politicians. Maybe Qadir had a point. Maybe they were all plain and simply venal, and he, with his high-minded principles, a tragic-comic figure on such a stage. He began to blub.

'If it's any consolation,' whispered Ferguson, 'they know that we were in Kayan and the location of the camp at Navor. I called them from Kamir's sat-phone when you two went out horse-riding.'

Chapter 15

The Kayan Valley was just like his home in Braelangwell on the east coast of Scotland, thought Ross. It was as if it had been transported halfway around the world, dry baked in a kiln, and deposited amongst the Hindu Kush. The barren hills rolled smoothly and the shepherds' paths cut across them like wisps of greying hair on an old brown head; the gullies, lying deep in the oblique dawn shadows, were etched into slopes like catheters.

He knew enough of the Ishmaelis not to anticipate early morning prayers, though he expected that from first light the valley would be astir with people utilising the coolest part of the daylight to its maximum. As he looked down, the place seemed as still as a graveyard.

He scanned the ground through his binoculars and with the improving light, saw that hardly a building remained untouched. Flat roofs had been punctured by artillery, drawing in the rafters like a spider's web heavy with dew; adobe walls had been blasted into dust leaving prickly crenellations, and black plumes of carbon streamed upwards from gaping windows like ebony keys on a piano. A broad mulberry tree, superficially wounded by shrapnel, bared its blanched teeth at the day. He descried amongst the rubble two – three – four corpses, one of them prostrate on the dirt highway with a brood of chickens pecking carefully around it. A little stain of darkness mushroomed out into the greyness at the stem of a pollard-willow tree, which leant mournfully towards the desolate scene. From it, a bloated body swayed gently in the lightest zephyr.

Though Ross had served in Bosnia and had witnessed first hand the razing of Muslim communities and villages, the atavistic hairs on the back of his neck stood on end at this first sighting of Kayan. He was a Ross, and in 1842 his clansmen had been burnt out of their crofts and massacred; a whole community razed to the ground as part of the infamous Highland Clearances, all in the name of 'Improvement'. *Was there no end to history, except an end in itself,* he wondered?

'Hello Two-Zero-Bravo, Two-Zero-Alpha – over,' said Ross into his throat-mike.

'Send, over,' said Jimmy Rothwell. Jimmy's team was five hundred yards to his east on a prominent spur from where he too had been picking over the bones of Kayan with vulture's eyes.

'It doesn't look good. Can you see any movement – over?'

'Nope. Just hens.'

'I'm going to take a look with Two-One Charley. You and Two-Two Charley stay put and be my eyes – Two-Two Charley, did you get that – over?'

'Yes – out,' replied Tommy Jessops, patrol leader of the western team of four.

It was half a mile down to the town across steep, rough ground, made trickier by the uncertainty of what may lay underfoot by way of mines, and also what they might find in the town. Every sense was keenly alert, and their heavy packs acted as a counterbalance against the slope. The four-man fighting patrol took up fire positions on the edge of the street looking north; the GPMG was set up on a red-earth bank affording the greatest killing zone, while Ross took up the point position with his signaller and 'runner' fanning out behind him on either side.

'Two-Zero Alpha; Two-Zero Bravo: I've got ya – over.'

'Roger – quiet so far – out.'

To call it a town was slightly over-egging it, thought Ross. It was nothing more than a ribbon development – some backward Mexican set up in a Spaghetti Western. He found the origins of the dark mushroom to be the smashed concrete trough beneath the mountain spring that had fed the town's mini-aqueduct and that now trickled out wastefully until it evaporated. The corpse that swung stiffly from the willow made gruesome viewing, with its pale blue pantaloons discoloured from massive bleeding. A desiccated, swollen tongue hung from the side of its mouth like a shot stag's. The eyes bulged, but even in death they had not entirely lost their owner's former lustre. The round, puffy face still seemed jocular; either mocking death, or finding some black humour in being sordidly hung up like a cured ham.

Flies gorged themselves on the macabre feast, wafting lazily from corpse to corpse and wound to wound on the half-dozen bodies around the tree. The faintly sweet, putrefying smell of rotting human flesh gave a clue to the massacre having been committed within a couple of days. It seemed to have been a search and destroy operation, with the victors bugging out as soon as it was over – certainly there was no evidence of them hanging around.

The building beside the spring still smouldered through its broken roof like a charcoal pit. Ross was curious to look inside, and advanced cautiously down its dim corridor. He presumed that it was some sort of hospice. It was neat and tidy, and had a monastic, sterile feel about it that was cool and serene. Bedrooms fed off the corridor. In each he found a single bed on which lay a single corpse, clinically butchered with bullets. Arms hung over the sides with sticky blood puddling beneath stiff fingers like a dropped rosary.

*

Bashir had arrived at Kayan on foot at dusk and oblivious to the massacre; a befuddled aching pain had reduced him to an automaton state of mind. On seeing the carnage that met him, his eyes had filled with tears, wondering that man could be so cruel. He had turned the few prostrate corpses that he came across without relief or joy that Walker and Ferguson were not amongst the dead. Then he had run, panic-stricken, through the once litter-free dusty street seeking sanctuary in familiar surroundings as a child does. Blindly he had found it in the ruins of Kamir's old home. He was starving. He found chocolate, biscuits and a bottle of beer; the first he had ever tasted. It began to take away his pain. He had another, then another and clasping his knees he had gently rocked himself to sleep.

In the morning his head throbbed as it had never done before. As sunshine began to fill the room, the flies mocked his weakness by darting sorties about his crusty eyelids. He got up with a start, not recognising the alien surroundings and frightened out of his wits, he dashed for cover behind the bar, the horror of his witness coming upon him with mortal dread. Then he was certain that he'd heard a voice outside – muffled and discrete – but a voice – an English voice.

The house was built into the slope, and set off from the street. He slithered silently on his belly to a shattered window and peered over the sill. He saw a big man standing over a corpse. The man was tall and broad, dressed in sandy coloured camouflage clothing, wearing chest-webbing painted in daubs of beige over the manufacturer's green garb. He was bareheaded, his hair matted dark with sweat. In the crook of his right arm he cradled a metallic-grey rifle that he had never seen the like of before. It looked neat and comfortable in the big man's holding.

'Two-Zero Bravo – nothing but the dead down here. Left in a hurry – over,' the big man seemingly spoke to himself.

Could it possibly be that the man was a friend of Piers? If so, why had he never mentioned him? Why appear as if a ghost in a graveyard? He wasn't Taliban – and yet he was definitely looking for someone or something. Bashir perceived that he had two immediate choices: to bide his time and risk discovery, or to gamble and give himself up? If – and it had seemed a hopeful if – if they were friends of Walker's then he may be able to help them, and if they were not

Taliban, what had he to lose? He had a third choice but it wasn't in his nature, so he left his AK-47 beside the window. Moving towards the door, he raised his hands high above his head and stepped into the day.

*

Robert Ross had sensed movement over his shoulder, but before he could turn he heard the shout from Trooper Finnigan with his GPMG pointing directly at whoever it was,

'Stand still!'

Bashir froze, petrified to the spot. He had not even contemplated that the big man was not alone. He was, after all just an interpreter. Ross swivelled and knelt on one knee, before adopting a fire position.

'Drop your weapon,' he barked in Dari.

'I – am – unarmed,' came a stilted reply in English.

'Keep coming,' he continued in Dari. 'Slowly now!' The wan-looking Afghan came gladly towards him and then stopped five-feet away. 'What's your name?'

'Bashir.'

'You speak English – how come?'

'It is my job. I am an interpreter from Kabul.' Ross lowered his rifle and frisked Bashir while the other three troopers covered him.

'What happened here?' he asked, indicating the bodies behind him.

'I do not know. I arrived last night.'

'Ishmaelis?' asked Ross, pointing to the dead at his feet.

'Yes.' Ross did not respond, his attention drawn to the steady stream of humanity cresting the hill to the south and now tracing a zigzag path down the slope like curious ants. Rothwell had spotted them too, and passed the information over the radio.

'Got 'em – out,' said Ross. 'Who are they?' he asked Bashir.

'I don't know. All I know is that these bodies are only a small part of the Kayan militia.'

'Vehicles coming from the east,' said Rothwell. 'Six of them. Pick-ups. Six in the back of each. Lightly armed but with RPGs. Moving about twenty miles per hour. With you in five – over.'

Ross looked at Bashir, 'Ishmaelis are anti-Taliban – right?' The Afghan nodded.

'Taliban left yesterday. They passed me at Mushi sixty miles south of here. I walked and hitched lifts between the two. There are no more.'

'Two-Zero Bravo – let 'em pass – out.'

'You British soldiers?' asked Bashir.

'Yes.'

'Are you friends of Piers Walker?' He had nothing to lose. Ross didn't flinch at the improbability of finding this information proffered so readily. The man was clearly scared; he spoke English.

'Was he here?' he rejoined curtly.

'He was. With Barry Ferguson. We moved to Mushi and then to Navor a week ago. They left me more than four days ago. They went alone with the rifle.' He was gabbling like a sinner at confession, hoping the very act would assuage his guilt and pain. 'They said if they didn't come back after two days I was to find Kamir.'

'Kamir?' he turned to look squarely at the Afghan. 'Is he here?' Again he pointed to the dead lying face down in the dirt.

'I don't know,' answered Bashir, shrugging his shoulders with an anguished, worn look on his face. He was frightened, surrounded by death and the prospect of it.

Ross turned to face the convoy again and then moved into the cover of a shattered building. Almost as an afterthought he dragged the bewildered Bashir with him by the collar. The convoy was four hundred metres away now.

The lead pick-up stopped and a virile-looking elderly man, short in stature, got out of the passenger side a hundred metres from Ross.

He had grey hair, sharp, clear blue eyes dug into a leathery face, and expansive moustaches like a warthog's tusks. The old man trembled as he stood by the open door of the cab. He staggered slowly from corpse to corpse, standing over each, rubbing his face besmirched with tears. He saw the figure dangling from the tree and broke into a faltering trot, gathering in the fawn tail of his pyjama suit as he ran. He shouted for help and stared up at the body. His shoulders jerked up and down, pushing out cries of anguish from deep within his soul. Tears poured down his lined cheeks. He threw himself at the feet of the mortal remains above him and beat the muddy earth, smearing it on to his chest.

'Fazir Khan… Kamir's father,' gasped Bashir, as the hanging corpse twisted round in a gentle wafting breeze.

Chapter 16

Their dark cell shuddered with the first explosions of the night. Walker had lost count of the number of nights like this one. The debris of plaster and dust rained down upon Walker and Ferguson. Excitement and fear gripped them as they looked up through their slit window like expectant children on Christmas Eve. Beads of orange tracer, like baked beans, crossed it momentarily and occasional bursts of phosphorescent light filled the room, after which an orange afterglow pervaded the cell like the flickering of a wood fire in a darkened room. The Kabul sky around their quarters was alight.

'It's begun again,' said Walker, squatting on his haunches like an Afghan, still chained to the wall.

Above the din of explosions and choruses of shouting outside, they discerned hurried footsteps approach their door before a tilly-lamp lit up the square aperture like an advent calendar. Keys rattled in the lock and the door was pushed open. Abdul Qadir crouched as he entered. His white garb acted like a movie-screen to the shadows playing around the room. He was followed by four al-Qa'eda gunmen who paired off against each prisoner and began to un-pick their locks.

'Good evening, gentlemen,' said Qadir, with theatrical politeness, as if enjoying the prospect of a play that he had scripted. 'Well now – I think that it is time we were moving on, don't you agree?' He rubbed his hands together as the prisoners were unshackled and then handcuffed again behind their backs.

'*The stars are setting and the caravan starts before the dawn of nothing – Oh make haste!* – eh, Mister Walker?' Ghoul-like in his white robes, his foxy features lit and shadowed by the lantern, Qadir chuckled to himself. Ferguson was non-plussed by the Arab with whom he had hardly exchanged a word, whilst Walker looked at him crossly. It had indeed begun.

*

Once out of the dungeon, polypropylene cement bags were thrust over their heads and masking tape wrapped around their eyes. Walker could sense the tension surrounding them in the low voices murmured close by. There were periodic moments of silence amidst the flinch-making bangs and shock waves of incoming ordnance. A timorous rat-a-tat-tat from the Taliban's archaic ZSU-232 anti-aircraft posts followed each blast.

Walker heard the garden gate creek. Unable to see where he was going he was ushered through in a more considered manner than had been usual. His captors spat a final admonishment at the kindly chowkidar who had often smiled sympathetically at him during his comings and goings. He heard the smooth action of a van's sliding door open, and then, somewhere very near to him, slammed shut, with an instruction in Dari to the driver who revved his engine petulantly.

He coughed as smoke from the exhaust gathered in his sack. It was immediately echoed from behind him by Ferguson. 'That's good,' he thought, 'we're still together.' He was rudely crammed into the back of a van in which he felt the press of stale, sweaty flesh on either side of him. He heard the clank of rifle barrels on the vehicle's aluminium frame. He was the filling in a particularly unappetising sandwich. The recent healing of his wounds was undone with the almost perceptible splitting of the soggy scar tissue about his thighs. Seeping crimson discoloured his beige pyjama bottoms, like the burst capillaries on a drunk's face. He shivered with pain.

Quietly he coughed again: silence. The door was rammed home. He coughed again: silence. 'Oh shit!' he thought. The front passenger door was closed smartly and the at-once-recognisable voice of Qadir, calm and collected, asked the driver:

'You know where to go?'

'Yes – to Botkhak…'

Piqued, Qadir cut him short: 'I only asked if you knew where you were going.'

'Botkhak,' thought Walker. He was amused by the chink of weakness in Qadir's self-control. Beneath that polished veneer he was rattled, nervous when realising the full force of American military intent. He was running now – but running to a plan.

Walker knew Botkhak to be east of Kabul, he knew the area from past excursions, but would he go north or south? Either way the Pakistan border was porous and lawless. As if able to read his mind, and rebuking it, Qadir turned to his hooded captive and said with a politely concealed sneer:

'You see Mr Walker – or perhaps you don't!' He laughed sardonically. 'The hubris of your American cousins could not be contained for long.' Walker remained silent. Qadir turned back and settled into his seat.

For several hours they withdrew, bumping along a pitted road. Each bump caused Walker's congealing wounds to separate from his plastic seat with excruciating pain, like that caused by the ripping of fabric from a blister. Their route was so circuitous, out of necessity as much as Qadir's deception, that it was impossible for Walker to mentally plot it. And then they stopped. He could sense that it was morning: the air was not so cool and the smells more certain; and there was the noise of animals in the near distance. A camel brayed and was joined in a chorus by more of his brethren, the ammoniac stench of their urine clinging to the dawn with vitriol. Several dogs growled as the doors of the vans were opened, and a cockerel beckoned the day. No one around him spoke, though some brought up phlegm from their innards with rasping ferocity and spat it upon the ground.

The driver drummed his steering wheel rhythmically whilst he surveyed the encampment of black and tan goatskin tents pinned to the ground by guy-ropes and rocks. A veil of mist lifted gently from the scrubby vegetation as eager sunbeams pulled the dampness from it. Fingers of smoke from wood fires clawed themselves above the veil and dissolved into the honey sky.

The womenfolk in highly-coloured dresses of reds, purples, yellows and greens, busied themselves around the cooking-fires, tending to the flames, whilst others began to break the first of the tents. Beautiful urchin-like children with eyes like saucers toddled and ran around the area chasing billy-kids and chickens. Some children went about topless; others wore mismatching pink, blue or green trousers with odd tunic dresses over them. A small boy in just his shirt-tails – a toddler only – stood sucking his thumb as his mother milked a goat, squatting on her haunches. Imperious-looking men in shawls, turbans and waistcoats wandered idly around their still-lying camels, their wooden kajawah – panniers – set off beside them. Half-heartedly the driver counted more than fifty camels littered about the camp's periphery; and perhaps thirty kuchi, though it was difficult to tell amidst the hotchpotch of tents. Angular grey-green hills towered above the scene.

Walker was dragged out of the van by his shirt collar without a word and stumbled to the ground. He was guided at each elbow as he walked unconfidently across the uneven ground; his head was bowed, expecting to be hit at any moment. He shuffled forty paces, stubbing his toes twice, the latter time causing him to cry out in pain. This was rejoined by a cuff on the back of his head from his escort. He was halted and turned around – one final twist for the unwilling participant of blind-man's buff, as if he were not disorientated enough already.

He was forced down to the ground by his shoulders, his coccyx hitting a hard jutting rock.

Then he heard giggling close by as he felt his hood pulled taut. Cold, sharp steel was pushed through his fibrous sheath. It jagged against his cheek, and then sawed a post box across his mouth. He was frozen with fear. A brown finger that stank of shit trailed over his lips accompanied by greater laughter. And then, as if feeding a diffident animal, a piece of naan was jammed into the opening. Walker smelt the bread; it was still warm. He snapped at it, wolfing it all into his mouth before chewing. He felt the rim of a plastic bottle touch his lips and willingly drank the cool spring water offered.

Walker judged the elapsed time only by forced rests and feedings, and guessed that they had travelled for two days since their flight from Kabul. Still bagged and bound, he had been placed on top of a recalcitrant mule and his hands tied to the pummel of the coarse-fibre saddle. He had learnt the hard way to anticipate the swaying movements of his carrier, falling innumerable times. His arms would be wrenched from his body as he was dragged along until the faltering escort of foot soldiers stopped the animal and replaced him on its reluctant back. No love was built up between man and beast, though as time went on there appeared to be understanding and some sympathy. The mule no longer hurried on to maximise the discomfort of his towed baggage when he fell, but stopped short and nuzzled him until the laughing militia caught up.

Almost at once Walker had picked up an unusual paradox about the extremists. Their spirits were evidently high as shown by the laughter that met each fall, but their field discipline, for Arabs and Afghans, was impeccable. He never heard anyone utter a single word. It was almost as if they were going about their business mechanically.

He had only the clue of Botkhak to hold onto and no inkling of their direction or the distance that they had travelled. That they went cross-country was axiomatic from the lack of extraneous chatter along the way, and that they travelled through mountain passes and gorges was also a given by the echoes of the mules' hooves and the tumbling of dislodged rocks rolling downhill. In addition, the air seemed cooler for long periods each day with only short perceptions of warmth in the middle. Fifteen miles a day would be going some, he reckoned, but guessed that they would be lucky to achieve half that pace. He also had no idea whether Ferguson was still with his group. Or indeed Qadir.

Separated from his comrade, Ferguson was faring no more comfortably. His long heavy body wasn't meant for riding a horse, let alone a smaller beast such as a mule. His bruises were bruised further by his initial capsizes, and his muscles strained from unnaturally morphing his senses to those of the mule. 'If I'd wanted to be a donkey-walloper, I'd have joined the sodding Household Cavalry,' he had chided inwardly at the start. But then as each faltering step merged into what seemed like eternity, so his mind began to ramble through disorientation, sleep deprivation and malnourishment. He began to lose the will to win even his personal battles. He stank of sweat, excrement and fear. He was at one with the beast.

There was a clatter of rocks. He felt the mule's outward hind leg pump furiously. The rigid silence of the trail was broken by anxious foreign cries. A swish of a cane breezed airily passed him twice; and then a third stroke cut viciously into his upper thigh. His cry of pain was lost in the expressed anguish of his carrier, its brutal eeyore echoing around the canyon. And then he experienced the sensation of free falling. A falsetto cry rang inside his bagged head. It was his own.

There was a sickening crack, followed at once by a piercing equine shriek. He landed heavily on his shoulder, and was pulled downwards, gaining velocity, losing all sensibility. He rolled twice, was pulled over twice, and then came to rest in a twisted mangled heap, his head resting on top of the mule's stomach. A calming fear seemed to have come over the beast. Its lungs gently lifted and fell, and a sonorous purring came from its mouth.

Ferguson was aware of the men. A mini-avalanche of scree had preceded them. An excitable chatter took place directly above his head. A moment of silence. He heard the click of an AK-47's safety catch being undone. He braced himself against the still mule. He jerked back at the impact of the three round volley, blood spurting and then seeping onto his grimy torso. He passed out.

Walker woke from a faltering sleep, crouched against a cold rock face and covered with a limp shawl. He jerked himself upright striking his head against the rock. It hadn't been a dream: it was still all so horribly real. He perceived a group of his inquisitors standing over him, and then his head was pulled forward and roughly bowed by the men. He felt the cold hard blade get underneath the masking tape and slice through it. There was an immediate rush of relief as the blood flowed more freely to his head. The bag was ripped from his head. He screwed up his eyes, blinded by the daylight. He blinked hard and through his flickering peep show descried the smiling, kindly face of Qadir looking into his.

'Excuse our little precautions will you Mr Walker, please. Though I am sure that a man like yourself will appreciate the necessity. We don't want too many people to know about you, do we?'

Walker looked blankly at him and then beyond, taking in the surroundings. He was at the bottom of a gorge, which was no more than ten-feet wide, cleaved between high, steep, almost vertical, escarpments. It was a short natural feature of only a couple of hundred yards length, in which, like a train parked in a siding, the caravan had halted for the night and was now active with its morning routine. The women, all of whom were unveiled, busied themselves around their small independent fires. A small boy advanced towards him bearing two opaque glasses and a billycan of steaming chai, and under one armpit he hugged two pieces of warm naan. He put his offering at Qadir's feet and silently turned away.

'Where's Ferguson?'

'Oh, he is in safe hands, just around the corner over there.' Qadir pointed to the first turn in the gorge some fifty yards away. 'He had a little problem with his transport.'

'Can I see him?' Qadir poured the tea.

'Hmm... Perhaps you shall, but all in good time, my friend,' hissed the serpentine master. 'All in good time. Now that we are in relative safety, life will be a little more comfortable for you.'

Walker looked down with self-pity at his handcuffed hands, his wrists swollen blue and purple with the battering of the journey.

'But not quite so comfortable,' smiled Qadir, following his hopeful eyes.

Walker looked to his right and saw a swarthy, squat Afghan squinting at him. His beady black eyes were burnt into a brown face crossed with the deep lines of his vocation. The man wore an open sheepskin coat with a threadbare crimson, floral pattern stained by the road. He carried a rifle slung over his left shoulder, and with his right hand he shook the dregs from his glass of sweet green chai. His hardwearing brown canvas trousers were tucked into knee-high leather boots like a trawler-man's.

Noting Walker's distraction, Qadir turned to his left. 'Ah, Iqbal – leader of this kuchi caravan. We hadn't told him exactly who you were – your paintwork is wearing a bit thin. He doesn't come across Caucasians that often.' He broke a piece of bread for him.

'Strange bedfellows for the Taliban, the kuchi?' questioned Walker, chewing painfully on the bread.

'Not really.'

'I mean, they aren't exactly adherents to the Taliban lore and ethics. They lend money after all, don't they? And their women – well look at them will you.' Qadir declined with monastic sanctimony.

'Ah, but there again there is more commonality than perhaps you see with your prejudicial we know best view of life. They are Pathans, the same as the Taliban. These are of the Ghilzai stock. They don't want Afghanistan, or Pakistan for that matter, to fall under Western suzerainty. You perhaps know the Pathan prayer: God, don't make me dependent on anyone.' Walker blew a horse-like affirmation through his crusty nostrils. 'And of course they have legendary valour.' He paused to look up to the high ridges with a smug grin. 'Do you know where we are, Mr Walker?'

'If my memory serves me correctly, this is the Tunghee-Tariki gorge. I stayed in Khubbar-i-Jubbar nine years ago when climbing near here.'

'I am impressed. Now let us see how good your history is…'

'The British were duped into accepting terms of a safe passage from Kabul to Jalalabad in the winter of our 1842. They were mostly butchered right here by the Ghilzais.'

Wistfully, Qadir looked again at the forbidding edifices. 'Yes, my friend Iqbal's forebears up there, popping off your forebears with their humble jezails.' The Arab made a childish imitation of firing up into the rocks, 'pop-popping' to himself, his eyes glazing over. 'Ah yes, the wheel of life turns, does it not, Mr Walker?'

'If you say so. But look where it's got you.'

Un-offended by this rebuke, Qadir smiled at Walker, stood up and ambled back to the senate of al-Qa'eda men deliberating over their breakfast around the dying embers of their own fire.

Iqbal advanced tentatively as if the captive were diseased or dangerous. He spat his naswah at Walker from five paces, landing a green globule of phlegm at his feet. 'American?' he asked hoarsely in pidgin English.

'British,' returned the prisoner in Dari, meeting his stare with defiance.

The little man took two steps forward and stood over the Scot. He yanked his matted beard, pulling his face towards his, and looked closely at his now obvious European features. 'I had hoped as much,' he said with vituperative satisfaction. 'And the other?' Walker tightened the muscles in his jaw. 'I know already – I can see it in your eyes,' he said, his voice schizophrenically adopting a softer tone and sensitivity, not matched by his pockmarked visage. 'Don't worry, my friend, the days of these curs,' he spat again, 'are numbered. Iqbal has a nose for such things.' He scraped his crow-like appendage with a crooked dirt-ingrained digit. 'And he always backs a winner.' He nodded sagely, dropped Walker's beard, and walked away, setting his eyes to their more usual cheerless shuttering.

Later that afternoon with the sun high above the valley that the gorge fanned into, Walker heard the faintest of droning noises overhead. If anyone else in the caravan had heard it they made no show of it, their heads and backs bent against the onward march. He looked up, narrowing his eyes to accommodate the brightness. He saw what looked for all the world to be a golden eagle; its wings spread rigid, drifting in a warm current of air, seeking out his prey.

The Raptor was indeed searching out the ground. Its almost supersonic propeller blades bit into the dense, cold high-altitude air above the valley, whilst the mechanical bird of prey returned a data stream of photography back to its base location. Walker turned his face towards it and bared his plaque-covered teeth with all the cheesiness that he could muster, and in doing so failed to notice the turn in the track, or anticipate his charge's lurch to the right. He was tumbled from the saddle and was dragged twenty yards imploring the mule to stop. The pain was a small price to pay for the exchange of hope that he had gained.

Chapter 17

On the morning of 13 November 2001, BBC correspondent, John Simpson, walked into Kabul ahead of the Northern Alliance. Just over two months after what had simply become known as 9/11, the Taliban had been all but vanquished. The capital had been liberated, and in the face of five years of repressed anger from Afghanistan's people, the former rulers had fled to their nominal capital Kandahar – or mostly to the four winds. The entangled web of al-Qa'eda had seemingly been destroyed, but without catching the spider. Though by its very loose, spectral nature, to knock out its several training camps was not to extirpate the nexus of terrorism. Whilst the world's media had fed the vengeful armchair generals back home amazing visceral scenes of retribution, the Americans and the British recognised that the '*War on Terror*' was merely completing the first of many untold laps.

Ross's Troop had had a quiet 'war'. Together with Fazir Khan's force they had held the Doshi intersect for re-supply from north to south and not fired a shot in anger. After the fall of Kabul, the troop had been picked up by helicopter and taken along with Bashir – now an honorary and invaluable member of the SAS Troop – to Bagram airbase pending future mop-up operations. At Bagram they had found that Squadron HQ had been established along with the three other troops. Tales of derring-do were swapped, along with deep-felt gripes at having been deployed as show-ponies to the world by their political masters.

Many of the troopers had never before seen action, and Ross's troop listened with gullible envy, and with reticence. Sure they'd had the kudos of being dropped in first, and had successfully teamed up with a tame anti-Taliban force, but they hadn't engaged with the enemy, and that's what counted amongst the testosterone brigade. They had been placed under strict orders to keep to themselves who and what they had unearthed in Navor, and so they were eager to demonstrate as much to themselves as to their comrades, their battle worthiness.

There were still plenty of heroic opportunities to be had as American Special Forces were pushing east, believing that they were hot on the trail of Osama bin Laden, now allegedly holed up in the Tora-Bora Mountains on the Afghan-Pakistan border. The squadrons were on a state of high alert.

Ross was writing a letter home to his girlfriend when the runner came into the hangar summoning him to the OC; he grabbed his rifle and followed behind. The HQ was a nine-by-nine tent erected within a hangar at the airbase and was connected to a short wheel based Land Rover otherwise ready to bug out at a moment's notice. The runner let him pass as he pushed his way through the capacious overlapping opening into a self-contained world of communications, light, and intelligence. There was a buzz from the comms equipment and the dulled throb of a generator running outside.

The OC, Freddie Wilson, a thirty-five-year-old Cambridge-educated former cavalry officer, was sitting lazily in a green canvas director's chair, his feet up on the operations desk and his radio handset pressed to one ear. With his free hand he scribbled notes dictated to him into a notebook. He acknowledged Ross with a friendly furrowing of his brow and indicated for him to pull up a chair beside him. Two signallers sat at the other end of the six-foot long table with all the paraphernalia of modern signalling mingling with the old and trusted logbooks open before them, pencils at the ready, sharpened at both ends. A large map of Afghanistan under a stiff plastic cover inscribed with coloured china-graph hieroglyphics dominated the fold-up table.

Harry Slim, the squadron's attached Intelligence Officer, strode into the ops tent and perched on the corner of the table next to the OC. He was a genial chap, though your typical egghead Int. Officer, thought Ross. His slight to medium build, neatly brushed wavy chestnut hair and rolled-gold-rimmed circular spectacles completed the stereotype in his mind. That said, there was more to him than met the eye. He was a supreme athlete, running marathons in sub-two hours and fifteen minutes; he was an able rock climber who had shown his mettle on exercises with the Mountain Troop; besides all of this he was human – a jolly self-deprecating sort. More importantly he had proved himself to be oftener right than wrong.

'You know Harry, don't you Robert?' asked Freddie, putting the handset back down on the table. Ross smiled at Harry. 'Harry's got a report from Kabul that they've found a house in the Shahre Naw district – the old embassy set up – where it is believed that two foreigners disguised as Afghans had been kept prisoner and tortured within the last two months.'

'What do you know?' asked Ross of Slim.

'Not a huge amount. Apparently the house was owned and often visited by Abdul Qadir – he's pretty high up in al-Qa'eda.'

'I know – go on.'

'The chowkidar is still there. He says that two ferangi were brought to the house and kept in the cellar. He says that they came just as the aid workers started leaving – that's around nine-eleven – and they left some time after the bombing started, but he doesn't recall which bombing.'

'Is he credible?'

'I'm coming to that. There certainly is a cellar in the house and it is geared up for keeping prisoners – rings in the walls, no real windows. Plus it stinks, and stinks of someone fairly recently inhabiting it. There's blood all over the walls.'

'So they could be dead – whoever they were?'

'The chowkidar, Kari Mullah is his name, says he saw them being evacuated. This Mullah, he's generally a silent type. Looks like a womble – and like a womble he seems to have picked up quite a lot of useful rubbish. These foreigners were apparently singled out for special treatment – taken out one at a time and returned a couple of hours later, beaten and bleeding across their backs. And then it stopped. That's when Qadir took more of an interest in the housemates.'

'How do you know it was Qadir?'

'Mugshots confirmed by Kari Mullah. Plus there's plenty of documentation to link him to the building – lease agreements, etc.'

'And who do you suppose these foreigners to be?'

'We don't. They were badly beaten up. Kari Mullah couldn't pick 'em out of the photos we showed him.'

'And how do you know they were foreign?'

'Kari Mullah heard the guards talking about them. All we have to go on is that one of them was bigger than the average Afghan. He didn't think that they were Pathans, despite their battered faces. But remember the guys we're interested in had integrated themselves into the population over a number of months.'

Freddie Wilson sat up in his seat. 'So Robert, what I want you to do is get down there with Bashir and take a look for yourself. Talk with this chowkidar. Bashir knows better than we what was in these guys' minds and more importantly what they looked like. Don't hang about though – we've got intelligence coming in from all over the place and can't afford too many wild goose chases. But if… if there is a chance of getting Walker and Ferguson back, we've got to take it.'

*

Later that night the three men reconvened in the ops tent.

'So what have we got, Harry?' asked Freddie Wilson, leaning back in his chair beside Robert Ross.

'Well, Freddie, we know that Walker and Ferguson were last seen for certain on around tenth September when Bashir left them in the Helmand irrigation system. We know what kit they had, their route and their intentions. We don't know their firing point.' Slim was indicating place names on the map using a whip antenna as a pointer.

'We know that Connor and Murphy were shot in the al-Qa'eda training camp – by whom is not known. We know that two intruders were caught by an al-Qa'eda patrol and brought into the camp on or around ninth or tenth September – when news broke of Massoud's assassination. We know that the training camp had been tipped off that someone was planning something and had been on alert. We also know that a weapon similar to a Barrett was brought in with the intruders. We pieced all this together from the camp-boy imprisoned and left to rot there.'

'Yeah, but you don't know that the two prisoners were Barry and Piers,' cut in Ross.

'True – we don't. They could be dead or hiding out. The latter seems unlikely. So far it points to our men. We also know that they were taken alive from the camp. Question – why? In addition, we know that Qadir had responsibility for setting up the training camp and was there on the tenth – this gives us a link to his house in Kabul.'

'How come you know that Qadir was running the camp?'

'Because intelligence linking al-Qa'eda to PIRA names him as the contact and organiser, and because the boy has picked him out from photos. His description of the guy pulling the strings before we showed him the photos matches Qadir anyway.'

'Seems a sensible assumption to me. So they were caught and taken alive to Kabul,' said Wilson, nibbling the top of his pen.

'Robert's found that the descriptions of the battered captives match those of Bashir. In addition, their arrival times in Kabul match departure times from Navor, loosely. Now we come to the interesting part.' He took from a loose-leaf cardboard folder half a dozen black and white aerial photographs, and laid them out on the table in front of the two SAS officers.

'We know from Kari Mullah that they left in a convoy of light coloured Hiace vans some time into the bombing campaign which started on seventh October. We don't know where they went, but we do know that Qadir was with them when it set off.' He drew their attention to the left hand picture.

'Shit – that's six weeks ago,' muttered Ross.

'Like I say – we don't know when they decamped. Now look at these – five vehicles parked up in the lee of this escarpment. Hiace vans abandoned. Satellite passes confirm they haven't been moved in days.' The OC and his troop leader leant forward to study them. 'We haven't any definite time of arrival for them, but it's no more than two weeks ago. Again, low-orbit satellite passes confirm this.' Ross' face lightened at this news.

'There's an obvious route into the hills here through the Khoord Kabul Pass,' continued the intelligence officer.

'The Jaws of Death,' mused Wilson.

'Nice,' said Ross, shifting his position and looking at his superior.

'The first ambush in the infamous retreat from Kabul in 1842. Thousands were slaughtered.'

'Well, we're on the same route here, Freddie, whether the same historical wavelength is a different matter. Look here,' he pointed to the third photograph in the line. 'Coming out of the Tunghee-Tariki Gorge is one half of what looks like a kuchi caravan. Nothing odd about that you might think, not for this time of year. But look more closely. Firstly, look at the ratio of men to animals – it's almost double the norm. Secondly, look at this guy on the mule emerging from the channel.' The two officers stared at the picture and then sat back like confounded schoolchildren. Slim smiled at them: 'He's looking up at something – no one else is. Also, he's on a mule – no one else is. Finally, he doesn't appear to be armed – everyone else that we can see has some sort of rifle over his shoulder.'

'Maybe he got sick or something.'

'Maybe. But look here at this satellite photo – this first one is from air recce by the way. You can see the caravan has moved on. Now look here – there's a second man (we presume a man) on another mule further back. The detail ain't so good obviously, but it confirms the ratio conundrum and that there are only two riders – the rest walk.'

'Why don't the Yanks blow them to pieces and ask questions later?' asked Ross.

'Because so far they aren't that interested. They reckon they're onto bin Laden in the Tora Bora. But whatever happens, their interest there will fade and they'll look for other targets.'

'And why don't we simply cut 'em up if you're so sure that Qadir is there and heading for the border.'

'Because there's a chance – a chance mind – that we can get Walker, Ferguson and Qadir alive.'

Wilson took up the conversational baton, 'We've got two days to try it our way. But it's sensitive, and so the softly-softly approach first off. We've got to keep the lid on Barry and Piers at all costs, and if the Yanks get a sniff of Qadir being in our sights – well those big American trophy hunters pulling the strings here could blow the whole thing in our face.' Wilson had stood up and was pacing the tiny enclosure, cogitating. After a moment he resumed, 'Robert, I want your guys to put a plan together for a covert recce. Harry will give you the latest satellite intelligence we've got – direction of travel, routes taken, speed, disposition and strength, times and latest positioning, etc. You'll have a QRF back up from here – heliborne. Any questions?'

'When do we leave?'

'When you're ready. But I want to go through the plan with you before you go. The only stipulation is a time to complete – you've got forty-eight hours from now.'

*

It took them nearly the full complement of twelve hours of darkness to cover their course, and when at last the dawn peeled back the night and scattered the clouds, Ross looked down from his OP into the valley. It was an angular defile cut out by mountain torrents feeding the headwaters of the Sorkab River, which ran into the Kabul River upstream of Jalalabad. A faint black stream snaked its way through the cutting, which looked a forbidding proposition from eight hundred metres above. The valley broadened a mile to the east where the hillside softened with terraced nut groves and fruit orchards stepped into it. Here, at its foot, the parched ground had a verdant tincture evident, above which – and on top of the spur – there hung a dozen spartan, flat-roofed adobe serais.

Ross had again split the troop into its four composite patrols – two in depth and two forward observing the valley, anticipating the caravan's progress. He had placed himself in the western position. He reached for the prestle switch,

'Hello Zero – this is Golf-Two-Zero Alpha, over.'

'Send – over.'

'In position now – over.'

'Roger – out.'

Davie Trott, a beefy blonde-haired West Country trooper of twenty-five with a face like a killer whale, smooth and round, but with a jutting jaw and rugged cheek bones, handed his troop leader a sachet of cold oatmeal porridge mixed with sugar.

'Cheers, Davie.'

'No probs, boss. How long before they appear do you reckon?'

'Who knows. If I were them I'd move at night, but the intelligence from the skies indicates otherwise. They'll pray now, at first light; eat and pack up, and be on the road before it gets too hot.'

'How do we know for sure that they ain't just a kuchi caravan?'

'We don't, Davie – we don't. The intelligence in this place hasn't been great so far has it, though Slim's done us good on other ops. That's why we're here – if Qadir is with them, then he, if anyone, will know where bin Laden is hanging out.' He ate some porridge, washing it down with a swig from his water bottle. 'You get your head down, I'm taking the first stag.'

Davie Trott gently shook Ross as the late morning sun began to eke out their position.

'Boss – there's movement to the west, coming round the corner.'

He slid from the natural cup in the ground to the edge and peered blearily into the valley. He was handed a pair of binoculars and watched as a squat little man emerged, peremptorily riding a scruffy mountain pony. He was followed by one – two – three camels, their kajavas laden with tents. Metal utensils dangled from their necks and glinted in the shadows that still filled half of the valley bottom. Hirsute men in rustic garb led the swaying camels, now numbering six. The brighter colours worn by the women and children dotted the train, with some of the children still sleeping on top of the bulbous kajavas across the camels' humps. Mules bearing cumbersome loads of hay and brushwood were interspersed with the camels.

Of the two supposed Britons riding mules there was no immediate sign, and save for the children and the leader all the men and women were on foot, the former sensibly armed with rifles slung over their shoulders. Every now and then the leader trotted back down the line to chat or to chivvy along the slothful, and though Ross could pick out the faces it was with no great surety.

The leader apart, one man stood out from the rest being more aloof. He walked alone with two men before him and two men behind so that in his white turban he looked like the middle spot of five on a dice. He walked with a pride and purpose unmatched by the caravan. His dress was altogether more urbane too, and apart from his white turban – which in itself was unique – his clothes seemed from afar to be cleaner, less drab than the rest. Around his waist he wore a pistol holster attached to his belt; oddly he wore combat-boots beneath his flowing robes. Shin high combat-boots, quite definitely. It must be Abdul Qadir – or was it simply that Ross wanted it to be him? From this distance he couldn't positively ID anyone.

One other man caught his eye, but only because he was taller than the rest. Unfortunately the man walked in a huddle on the far side of the line and only the top of his head could be picked out, and on this he wore a cream Chitrali cap pulled down at the back. As the caravan sashayed towards them, Ross counted sixty-five people, of whom forty-five were men. They watched it pass until it disappeared beyond the village two miles on, and at last the sun lit up the whole of the valley. It was 1 p.m.

'Hello Zero – this is Golf Two-Zero-Alpha – over.'

'Send – over.' Ross sent a succinct sitrep of what he had witnessed, adding that no one was following the caravan. 'We're going to watch them settle in for the night as planned – over.'

'Roger – out.'

The troop settled down in their four positions waiting for nightfall and their next move. Rothwell's team was to the rear looking back on the path of their insertion. He'd heard Ross's sitrep and knew that they would have a longish wait before the close recce reported back. The foxhole in which his team of four sheltered from the icy air was a sangar of boulders pulled from the ground and camouflaged with clods of brown permafrosted earth. The GPMG was set on the killing zone of the path. 'Pepe' McEwan, a Glaswegian with an Italian mother, handed him a steaming cup of coffee from his flask. He took his gloves off and cupped it gratefully, holding it close to his face so that the steam warmed his cheeks. He sipped it and passed it back.

'Cheers, Pepe. It'll be a bloody cold night, I reckon.'

'Aye, it's been a bloody bitter day even with the sun on our backs.' The trooper passed the cup to his neighbour. Jimmy Rothwell sat contemplatively, watching the last of the daylight disappear, his night vision sight resting in his lap. 'What you thinking about, Jimmy?' asked the Scot.

'Nothing much... but then again everything, I suppose. The beginning... the end. Those two down there— '

'If it is them.'

'Aye, well that's as may be. We've been through a lot together one way or another. They were always deep – in their own ways, of course. Kind, meticulous, ruthless even. Bloody good sorts. Never wanted of a better officer. An' look where it got 'em.' A movement, barely discernible in the half-light, distracted him. He put his sight to it, and picked out a mountain hare darting into a tract of dead ground. He smiled to himself. It was just the sort of thing that Walker had always spotted and tried to get others to take an interest in. He put the sight back in his lap.

'I guess it got 'em exactly to the same position as we are, eh?' rejoined Pepe with the wisdom of Job.

'Except that we ain't been cuffed and battered like a fried haggis puddin' from a fish bar on Argyle Street, 'ave we, eh Pepe?'

'No – no we haven't. Not yet anyway.' He looked at the sergeant, five years his senior, deep in thought, searching out the darkness. 'You're not such a shallow pool yoursel', you know,' said the Scot mockingly. Shaken from his reveries, Rothwell gave him a friendly cuff about the ears.

'Now let's get young Toddy up for his stag shall we, and start thinking about stand-to and then the night-time routine.'

*

Bashir strolled down the valley as the day drew to its close, seemingly without a care in the world. He selected from the tied napkin in his pocket a dried mulberry, a toot. The evidence of the caravan was abundant on the track, including the pungent smell of their goats, which had churned the dusty earth with their cloven feet and blistered it with puddles of urine. Kuchi women were by nature fastidiously miserly in retrieving the camel dung to use as fuel, but here and there, like cairns on a Highland track, he saw that they had missed a pile or two.

The dusk fell quickly. He could smell the tinder and dung of the cooking fires up ahead, though he couldn't see or hear anything yet. *Perhaps around the next corner*, he thought. An atavistic impulse from his youth electrified his senses and desire. Now was the time for guile, which was in his blood, if not his nature. He had to hide himself amongst the camp, seeking friendship with the shadows of the night. He stopped to pray before it was completely dark, laying out his petou in front of him. He was serenely calm and mentally strong.

He offered his soulful thoughts to a higher place, asking for guidance in the hours ahead. Especially, he pleaded for the safety of Walker and Ferguson; that he should find them alive, and lead them away from danger – though it was they who had led him into it. He espoused their good natures, even as unbelievers of the Faith, and prayed that Allah would be merciful. Once complete, he wrapped himself neatly in his petou and sat quietly down to a meagre supper of naan and toot.

Clinging to the spur above him, silhouetted against the dusk, a parade of ragged, short-staffed flags hung limply. Jutting slabs of roughly hewn stonework, like tar-stained teeth, protruded over the villagers' graveyard. In the distance a mongrel barked indiscriminately, accompanied by a burst of clucking from the chickens and one final, magnificent *cock-a-doodle-doo* from a rooster, bidding goodnight to all that had ears to hear him.

Meanwhile, Robert Ross sat huddled in his sangar straining his eyes in the fading apricot light. It was a battle he would not win, and reluctantly he put away his novel – Evelyn Waugh's *Men at Arms*. He had read the trilogy three times before, but still the 'Uncles' fascinated him. Since his first reading he had noted that nearly every Officers' mess had at least an Apthorpe amongst their number.

'Good book, boss?' enquired Davie Trott, passing his officer a cup of tepid tea, the last of his flask.

'Not too bad. Ah, thanks Davie. You had some?' The burly trooper nodded.

'We ain't seen no one all day long, 'ave we, boss?'

'No. I wasn't expecting to unless of course we'd stumbled on them. Al-Qa'eda are running like rats. Still, I suppose that we'd better stand-to, eh?' He picked up his G-3 and took up his fire position so that the five-man team were looking outwards over 360°.

His thoughts were with Bashir. It had been the obvious thing to do, to send him into the camp to see who was amongst the train. It was why he had brought him on the mission. He admired the little Afghan's pluck, and trusted entirely that he would complete the task if at all possible. It was evident that he adored Walker, and by all accounts Walker was a man who deserved the respect of anyone with whom he had had dealings. Ross felt a pang of guilt, which he quickly dispelled.

It was his job and he would see it through. If they could snatch Walker and Ferguson alive – so much the better. But Qadir was the jewel. To get him alive would perhaps ensure the safety of countless others. Politically it would be a coup for the 'War on Terror' and especially for the British. The little Afghan was down there pining for his lost friend, hoping against hope that he would be saved by Ross and his men. He didn't understand the bigger picture – how could he? He lived, had always lived, in a small, parochial world. One that had been destroyed by the internal and external machinations of self-interested groupings – and was being used again. Now he was being used. The mission was all-important to Ross, and if – if they could get their old comrades out alive as well... He looked at his watch.

'Right – stand-down lads,' he whispered and crept back into the pit.

'Another day at the office closes,' suggested Davie Trott quietly.

'Better get your head down, Davie. Bashir won't be back for at least four hours. Smithy and Dodsworth'll take the first stag.' He pulled the hood of his smock over his head, pulled his green Arab headscarf tighter around his neck and face, and hugged himself.

'*What a bloody load of shite,*' thought Ross. It wasn't just another day at the office. He knew – they knew – the people down there – Bashir, Walker, Ferguson. And they were depending on him. That made it different. But in his own simple way, Trottie was right – it was just a job – his job, and he loved it.

Chapter 18

Barry Ferguson was at an all time low. With shuffling, faltering steps he had been hidden amongst his guards at the rear, his head kept submissively bowed. His tied wrists hurt like hell; the swelling had long since broken and they now showed the first signs of septicaemia. A kuchi harridan had kindly sprinkled a mysterious powder onto his wounds. She had wrapped them in cooling wet rags, smiling as she did so with only a single tooth showing in her repulsive, malnourished mouth. He hadn't been able to raise a murmur of appreciation in his face. His cheeks were hollow, his beard patchy where it had once been full, and his eyes ached as if sunk in the coldest water imaginable. He had the shits since leaving Kabul and his frame had atrophied; he could keep nothing down – every mouthful, every swig of water fed the intestinal rodent gnawing within him.

He was kept apart from Walker, who seemed stronger than he when he glimpsed him at the front; he seemed conditioned to the way of life, able to engage with the rhythms of the caravan and its people even as its captive. He noticed that Qadir was sometimes with him, and that there was some kind of mutual respect between them. Or was it a symbiotic energy that fed from each other's desperate situation? He couldn't fathom it.

He sat down with his back slouched against the rockface; it was wet and slimy. He didn't care. He saw no poetry in it where Walker might have perceived the mountains to be weeping for them. He was drowning in his own self-pity, his dusty, throbbing head lolling on a forearm laid across his knees. Beside him the goats clattered, bumping each other playfully to secure their favoured spots to squat for the night.

He thought of home, of the sheep being gathered from the hills for their winter pasture, much as these God-forsaken nomads were doing with their livestock. He thought of his father with his feet up in front of a warm peat fire, a glass of whisky resting on the arm of his easy chair, and a book in one hand. His mother would be sitting opposite him, alternately knitting and staring into the fire, perhaps wondering where he was. He promised himself that if ever he got out of Afghanistan alive he would leave the army for good and work his father's farm. He fell asleep.

He felt himself being pulled gently. He lifted his head subconsciously. A benign, sympathetic face from his past – an Afghan face – looked deep into his yellow eyes, imploring his soul to steel itself. His head rolled back onto his arm and returned to a semi-comatose state.

In the mouth of a cave further along the defile, a fire burned brightly, dancing around the bearded faces of the kuchi men engrossed like little children in storytelling. On the opposite side of the narrow canyon sat another, more sombre, group of men around their own campfire. The man in the white turban sat at the head of their elliptical arrangement, and selected the choicest cuts from the plate of victuals. These men were different in their manners, their dress – altogether more puritanical than the road-weary kuchi, and they were mostly not Afghans, evident in their physiognomy caught in the firelight, and in their dialect. He guessed that they were Arabs. When the man in the white turban spoke the others listened, hanging on his every word like unctuous schoolboys. He had a presence; physically lean, no stronger than the rest, but it was clear that his intellect was above that of his followers.

Bashir couldn't be sure that it was Qadir, as he had never seen him in the flesh, but whoever he was, the man was the leader of this enclave of fleeing al-Qa'eda militia. He hung back in the shadows of the hairy goatskin tents created by the jumping flames. A ghostly half moon peered through succeeding sepia banks of cirrus clouds.

Security had been poor. It had been easy to evade the first two sentries he had seen as they had been more interested in the peep show of the veiled moon than in their sentinel duties. Those supposedly guarding Ferguson had been asleep. Now he was in the midst of the camp with only Walker to find. He had counted all but six men, and had guessed that the women and children were tucked away in their tents. He presumed that there must be another sentry position at the far end and Walker was likely to be with it.

Not knowing the layout of the camp and being unable to see it in its entirety, he had decided that boldness best suited his designs and so he strode through it. He passed the fire of the kuchi men and heard Iqbal in full flow,

'What need have we for time? The seasons and our bellies move us. The West – they are obsessed with time, and filling it. With what? It is as though they are manacled to time…'

'But they are,' cut in a deep voice. It was accompanied by a man's arm being thrust into the firelight, with his other hand mimicking a wristwatch. This was met with uproarious laughter. 'It's as if in their ambition to capture time in a little disc, they have been caught by it.' A spark shot up into the night, lighting up the periphery and picking out Bashir looking guiltily into the reverie.

With friendly intent Iqbal beckoned for him to come forward: 'Come and join us, friend. We were just talking about time, and how much there is of it, and of how much there is wasted in trying to keep it…'

Bashir looked embarrassed and played dumb.

Iqbal turned back to his group and said with contempt, 'They too think they are so damned superior, these wretched Arabs.' He spat into the fire as the kuchi men giggled loudly. Bashir slunk back into the shadows and moved on.

He picked his way through the camp with the aid of the glow from five independent fires, which silhouetted the nomads' open-ended tents. Long poles, tied to supporting rafters at the top of the tents' wooden frames gave them the appearance of spokes in a bicycle wheel. Within them, black bodies occasionally tossed, coughed and spluttered in the darkness. A camel gave out a long, rumbling belch that made the timid Afghan more nervous as he sought out his old friend.

He stopped by the last tent and listened to the chatter of the eastern pickets. He could hear four voices talking in an alien tongue. His heart leapt as he heard a voice filled with humour and familiarity begging, in Dari, to be heard by his guards.

'Abu Iglin!' cried Walker with mock discomfort.

'What do you want you cur?' replied a bark from the darkness.

'To take a piss, you bastard.'

'OK my friend, nanny will be with you presently.' The three guards, though not knowing what had been said in Dari, joined in Abu Iglin's chuckling.

'*Typical Piers*,' thought Bashir. His knack of getting on with people in any situation was uncanny. It was as though he were a princeling guest of the al-Qa'eda rather than their prisoner.

It was a façade though. Deep inside, Walker longed for it to be over. He knew that the Americans, and perhaps the British, had already begun their retaliation. But he had no idea how quickly the Taliban might topple. As no military activity had been evident during their flight from Kabul into the mountains, perhaps the portents of 1842 that Qadir had invoked would – or were coming – to realisation. Where they were going to and where it would end he had no idea; he had nothing to hope for save that Hereford had known that they had been alive before Massoud had been assassinated, and that the Raptor had been looking for and spotted him.

Bashir's impulse had been to go to Walker and to offer words of encouragement; instead he smiled to himself and thought, '*He's alright,*' and stole away into the blackness, leaving Walker to his performance.

*

As the morning fires were lit, the azan was called and the group of Arabs gathered to prostrate themselves on the barren valley floor like a set of dominoes, whilst the kuchi went about their morning rituals with equal reverence. It was a cold pink dawn and the dew was heavy on the goatskin tents. A toddler, naked from his waist down, peed on the ground at the edge of the camp at the same time as picking his nose, a habit he performed with greater interest.

Iqbal was having his breakfast beside his tent: a hard-boiled egg, some warm naan and a glass of chai. He was watching the boy with disinterest, but allowed himself a smile as he noticed Qadir shoot a scornful half-glance at the little urchin. *'You should be concentrating on your prayers, my foxy friend,'* he thought to himself as he pushed the remnants of his egg into his mouth.

Iqbal was about to get up when he saw the boy staring, transfixed, up into the hills. The boy turned suddenly, piss still streaming out of him and cascading down his filthy brown leg like a golden shower. He wasn't picking his nose anymore. His eyes were wide with fear; he was mouthing for his mother, but his throat was dry.

Like a sprinter from his blocks, Qadir leapt forward, grabbing his Kalashnikov, which he had laid in front of him like a dessert spoon. He cried out to his men to follow suit as he ran for the cover of the caves that the kuchi men had sat up in the previous night.

A maelstrom of bullets kicked up dirt around the Arabs and ricochets sang around the rocky cradle. Women clutched their children to their breasts, others howled and cried out for their offspring to stay still or to find cover. The kuchi men crouched beside their startled camels, completely taken aback by what was beginning to unfold.

Goats broke free from their jute tethers, kicking wildly as they rushed through the camp, upsetting pots of steaming water and bringing down tents.

Iqbal's first instinct had been one of self-preservation, but when he had seen Qadir weaving his way towards his tent, rifle in hand and screaming at his followers, he closed his eyes and stuck out his right leg. The timing and contact could not have been surer. Qadir was sent sailing through the air, the wind knocked out of him as he landed in a heap. Iqbal launched himself at the crumpled figure, holding him tight around the neck.

'You think you can treat us like curs, you superior bastard, huh – do you?' he shouted into Qadir's ear through clenched teeth. He jerked his grip on him harder, forcing a strained squeak from the Arab. Qadir's eyes bulged. He was choking, turning puce in the act of dying.

Behind Iqbal the goatskin tent collapsed as an al-Qa'eda gunman fell through it, lifeless. Iqbal turned, releasing his grip momentarily as he did so, allowing Qadir to prise the kuchi's arm briefly away from his throat.

'Get off me you fool,' gasped Qadir. 'Can't you see we're on the same—'

Iqbal regained control of the situation, throttling the Arab with greater severity. 'No – no we are not on the same side. You brought this upon yourselves – Iqbal looks after his own,' he snarled.

Qadir pointed his right elbow and aimed it powerfully into the Ghilzai's solar plexus. Iqbal cried out in pain and briefly relaxed his hold. It was all that Qadir needed, spinning free onto his knees. He grabbed the barrel of his rifle from the ground and swung it with all his might across the still dazed Iqbal's temples, toppling him to the floor.

Walker and Ferguson had been tossed up in the storm like flotsam, and dragged into the redoubt of caves by the Arabs. Both men found that they were suddenly resuscitated by the immediate and violent threat to their lives. Neither of them saw who, what or how this precipitation of destruction had been thrown at them, but both welcomed it like farmers rejoice at rain after a long drought. After so many solitary days they were again forced together, cowering behind a rock whilst their captors fought an unseen enemy. Many lay dead or dying on the ground outside; Walker had seen that at least five hadn't got up from their prayers, and had instead gone to sit at Allah's right hand as chosen Shadid.

There were half a dozen Arab fighters – including Qadir – in their cave, returning fire with little aptitude or self-control. Walker could hear shots coming from left and right in the adjacent caves, but he daren't look up. He struggled vainly to free his hands from their rope ties. Qadir seemed cool and peremptory under fire, as though enjoying himself greatly, willing the eye of the storm to twist around him. Cries of *'Allah Akbhar!'* reverberated like ululating women.

An Arab spun round and fell to the floor as a dead weight. Half his skull had been mashed and coarse yellow-white bone mixed with the bloody pulp like poor quality mincemeat. It oozed from the victim and seeped towards Walker's outstretched leg. Qadir shot the corpse a disdainful glare. Madness streaked across his face from those foxy-eyes, which were now intoxicated with lust for this orgy of martyrdom. Walker raised himself slightly.

'Stay down!' barked Qadir. He pushed the former SAS officer down with the heel of his boot, and then ordered two of his men to cover the Britons.

The wild shrieks turned to high-pitched cries of pain and anxiety as the firefight grew in intensity. Walker sensed it drawing ever closer to him. Ferguson too sensed its climax and attempted to bring it to a swifter conclusion. Like a prop forward going down into a scrum, he lunged at Qadir with all his might. The guard, seeing him launch, found Ferguson's face with a swift hard kick and then, with a sickening crunch, brought the butt of his rifle slamming down onto the bridge of his nose. The old war-horse lay motionless where he had fallen.

First one, and then the last of Qadir's front line force were dropped, each of them as they had attempted to reload. Qadir retreated to the depths of the cave, only five yards back, and drew his pistol. Now he was like a savage beast trapped by his hunters. He grimaced as he looked spitefully at Walker who was at the feet of the only other al-Qa'eda survivor. He heard the thudding rotor blades of helicopters beating nearer and nearer like a drum roll, echoing round the defile and escaping into the cul-de-sac of the cave. Qadir levelled his pistol at Walker's head.

*

'Any more questions?' asked Ross as he completed his orders high above the valley. Bashir had reported the news that Walker and Ferguson were definitely captives of the caravan, and that the likelihood was that Qadir was amongst them also. He had drawn a sketch of the layout from memory and given a detailed description to the troop commander whilst huddled in a makeshift sangar. The news had been swiftly relayed to HQ with the suggestion of a co-ordinated attempt to snatch Qadir at dawn. It had been a straightforward plan – the best ones always are.

Jessops' team would provide depth, covering fire and co-ordination from the high ground from where communications back to HQ were proven. Bashir would lead the remaining two groups into cut-off positions at either end of the kuchi encampment, spread over two hundred and fifty yards.

The mission was simple – to snatch Qadir alive.

Collateral damage was to be avoided but anyone who fought back was to be taken out. If, and Ross meant if, at all possible Walker and Ferguson were to be saved. As the faithful prayed soon after the azan, the patrols would move in to take Qadir. Heliborne reinforcements would drop at each end of the camp and move through to secure the position.

After the cold, bright and airless day spent hunkered down beneath the rough-hewn brown peaks, pocked with snow, and another bitter night on the peaks, the troop were eager for the fray.

Ross noted the sullen, sad veil come over the little Afghan as the troop dispersed into their fighting groups. He just sat where he was, staring blankly at his sketch.

'You gotta minute, Bashir?' He raised his head slightly; his brown eyes glazed with disappointment and weariness, but did not look at the officer. 'We've got to do this my way. If we get Qadir alive – many will be saved. And maybe – just maybe – we'll get Walker and Ferguson out too.' He paused. 'We want them out of there as much as you do.' He smiled a kindly, warm, but immovable smile. 'You understand?' He placed a large powerful hand on the bony shoulder of the gnome-like Afghan.

Bashir understood. He understood all too well.

The cut-offs crept silently into their positions and waited for dawn and the signal of the azan. As the sky lightened both Ross at one end and Rothwell at the other, fifty yards from the peripheries, perceived a problem – they were looking obliquely across the camp and couldn't pick out their targets. Ross looked searchingly at Bashir who was crouched beside him like a gun dog. He had his AK-47 held firmly in both hands and a tired and forlorn look in his eyes from the strain of lack of sleep and responsibility. He was frightened. He had never killed a man before and he clung hopefully to the strength and confidence of the British force, desperate not to be cast adrift. He looked up at the officer, shrugged his shoulders and shook his head apologetically.

A small boy bereft of trousers and still half-asleep toddled towards them, rubbing his eyes with one grubby hand and holding his penis in the other. Behind him Ross could see half of two lines of men bent forward on their knees in prayer. He thought he could make out a glimpse of white turban over the angled shoulder of one of the pious

Arabs. The boy stopped and began to pee, yellow spurts drumming the hard floor.

'*You need to take on board more fluid, sunshine,*' thought Ross. Beside him Bashir craned his head forward to see around the corner. The boy, who was looking straight at them now, spotted the slight movement of Bashir's head. He turned towards the camp, running and swerving through the faithful, now keenly alert. Qadir – Ross now saw that it was him – reached for his rifle.

The Troop had planned for this eventuality. The six men of Ross's section opened up on the terrorists without instruction from their commander. Five Arabs never got up. Panic was the most potent response as the others ran blindly into Rothwell's ambush.

'Zero – Golf-Two-Zero Alpha – Contact – over.' Ross spoke calmly into his throat mike as though commentating on a cricket match. There was no response. He didn't try again. Jessops would already have called for the QRF. He lost sight of Qadir.

The terrorists began to regroup and now returned fire with wildly inaccurate and ill-disciplined bursts, which pinged around the narrow confines.

'Go! Go! Go!' screamed Ross at the top of his voice and two four-man teams sprung forward into the open, one from either end of the ambush, supported by a crescendo of fire zoning in on the epicentre of resistance amongst the caves opposite.

The patrols scythed through the chaos, completely focused on their mission.

'Not 'ere!' came successive shouts from the open ground.

Jimmy Rothwell watched the action from his fire-support position, controlling the rate of fire and targets. It was like being back at Junior Brecon. He had seen two bodies being dragged into the middle of three caves by a pair of Arabs. With Ross's forces fire-and-moving amongst the dilapidated tents, the battle was engaged now on both sides of the defile.

It was a gut instinct decision, but he had to take action in order to save time – to save lives. Not only were the troopers on the ground exposed but so far their former comrades had evaded them: were they in the caves? He ran away from the firefight, and then tacked back onto the wall opposite his own men. He threw himself against it lest there be any unseen resistance. He could see now that there were more than a dozen dead Arabs, mostly lying where they had prayed, but there was also plenty of cover amongst the half-cocked nomad canopies.

He reached into his jacket for a stun-grenade, and leopard crawled to the side of the cave nearest to him. He could see the jerking muzzle flashes and hear the foreign cries from within.

'These fuckers want to die,' he thought.

The intensity of incoming fire into the cave nearest to him mounted. Ross's fire support group had discerned his intentions, and were now chipping and powdering the rock face, sending ricochets zinging past him. He lifted himself with agility, steadying himself on the balls of his toes. He pulled the pin and tossed the grenade into the cave yelling out 'Grenade!' as he let fly.

The boom was immense in that tight space. The firing stopped. In the same instant he leapt up, put his G-3 to his shoulder and sent two rounds into the shocked Arabs lying on their backs still clutching their weapons.

The firefight once again resumed from behind him. He looked back to Ross's section, his white teeth evident in the broad grin against his brown camouflaged face. Ross raised two fingers at him and jabbed towards the next cave.

'*What the hell did he mean: two terrorists or two prisoners?*' He had seen the two bodies being dragged into this cave but assumed that they were wounded Arabs. He changed his magazine. The firing from within the cave stopped. He pulled his G-3 into his shoulder again – '*'Ere we fuckin' go!*' He spun into the entrance, dropping to one knee.

It was a split second decision. He saw three men alive within, two of which were armed. One of them had a pistol; he wasn't pointing it at him. The other lurked in the background with his rifle. He was jabbering, having lost the will to fight. The upper lip of the man with the pistol was turned into a sadistic smile of sorts – he could see this even through his beard. At his feet quivered a wretched looking man. The gunman was startled as the SAS Sergeant appeared from nowhere into his peripheral vision. He turned his head slightly. Rothwell fired a double tap into his forehead. The Arab staggered back and withered to the ground. The man with the rifle gasped in horror, threw down his weapon, and flung his arms up into the air.

THE END

Epilogue

It was raining. It seemed to have been raining all that January. Piers Walker sat on the grassy shelf watching the River Teviot, absorbed by its gently rhythmic noises and its vibrancy. Raindrops splashed onto its cracked, peaty-black surface, which carried the extending ripples to the end of the pool. It was here, as in many places along its circuitous path that the river's lifeblood battled with the immovable defences of the river's foundations before moving elegantly on. Walker thought particularly of his friend Kamir and their chat about the Mullahs versus the Modernisers in Afghanistan. He had thought about Kamir a lot of late. In fact these days he thought of little else save the events of six months previously.

He was past chastising himself for causing Kamir's death. Kamir lived in a dangerous country and his equally dangerous vocation had brought with it many enemies. He'd have met his end soon enough, in much the same fashion. But still he mourned his old friend.

He'd not seen Ferguson since their return, but every week he learnt from his parents of his slow recovery. His skull had been fractured in two places and the bridge of his nose smashed – it had been an ugly boxer's nose anyway, or so he had told him when he'd emerged from unconsciousness in Islamabad. Septicaemia had set in about his wounds, and his atrophied body was only now beginning to fill out again. In short, he'd been lucky to be brought out alive.

Ferguson hadn't been well enough to attend the debriefing with the Director of Special Forces and his cronies, which Walker had been to in London. It had been a very polite and good-humoured discourse, though Franklin had looked embarrassed throughout, hoping to avoid the awkward topic of his murky subterfuge. Walker was too professional to have made a scene in public, but on the session breaking up he had left Franklin in no doubt as to the strength of his feelings. Franklin had apologised, and congratulated him on the job's total success as far as he was concerned – Qadir and the bonus of Connor and Murphy, all dead. But Franklin had taunted him, in a kindly, subtle fashion and the taunt hadn't left him since: *'Would he do it again, if he'd known what he was really supposed to do?'*

Undoubtedly not. But – *'Would he have gone out with Ferguson alone to kill Connor and Murphy again, as he knew the facts to be from the outset?'* Well, 'yes' and 'no'. Then, when presented with the circumstances he had decided to go with him. Now, having quashed the self-destructive urge to prove himself to himself – no, he wouldn't. Yet, therein lay his dichotomy – it was all right for him to take the law into his own hands to avenge a murder more than a decade ago, but not for him to do his government's dirty work when no longer in their employ. He had no answer to it, and nor did he care any longer to search for one. It was finished.

'But what had they actually achieved?' The two men that they had set out to kill had been killed – *'but, to what end?'* The IRA would find equally iniquitous bedfellows with whom to swap dirty tricks. And again, *'Did they feel any satisfaction in having watched their gruesome end? They might as well have been beside their hospital bed as they slipped away, surely?'* To this nagging self-doubt, he felt that in time they would feel that it had been personally worth it, though at some physical and mental cost to them and their comrades along the way. Kamir and Khalil had both been summarily killed along with many of Kamir's men. Bashir had survived to modestly tell the tale, and was now helping the Allies to rebuild his country. He, it seemed, and perhaps his homeland, had taken something positive from the last six months.

Above all else it had made Walker thankful to be alive. Thankful for what he had – to be living in the bosom of his family, surrounded by their lands, wealth, people. The cementing of this discernible fact within his psyche, well that was at least something. He was alive and intended to stay that way.

And Jenny. She had gone. She didn't understand – perhaps she never did. Or perhaps he never let her understand him. She'd felt betrayed and unwanted. A second thought to him – maybe not even that. She didn't even know where or why he'd gone in the end, just that he was going – had to go – and that he'd be back. She'd waited for two months, hoping that this was simply one last ego trip before settling down with her; she was sadly, uncontrollably disabused and had packed her bags and left at the end of the winter term. He hadn't bothered to contact her since his return. He had no ties, or so he arrogantly thought. He liked it that way. Life was straightforward.

He picked up his fly-rod, checked the heavy homemade yellow-haired tube-fly, and methodically cast across the water. At the limit of his reach, he quietly stepped into the river.